Where the Ground Meets the Sky

by Jacqueline Davies

MARSHALL CAVENDISH • NEW YORK

Acknowledgments
The author wishes to thank the following people: Gaby Peierls Gross and Jane
Flanders Ziff, both children of Los Alamos, for reading the manuscript and
generously offering their rich memories of life on the Hill; Robert Crockett, for
sharing his expertise on amateur radio during World War II; the Los Alamos
Historical Society, for fulfilling its mission so ably; Jane Yolen, for reading an
early draft and pointing me in the direction of Judith Whipple; Judith Whipple for
her unerring editorial direction; the Society of Children's Book Writers and
Illustrators, for awarding this manuscript its 1998 General Works-in-Progress
Grant; Ann Davies, for all those Saturday lunches; Susan Davis, for reviewing the
scientific information in the Author's Note; and all the members of the First
Monday Writers Group. I'd especially like to thank my first readers, Monica
Driscoll Beatty, Tony Helies, and Christie Allan-Piper, for their early criticism and
unfailing support—a most heartfelt "thank-you."

Marshall Cavendish, 99 White Plains Road, Tarrytown, NY 10591

Library of Congress Cataloging-in-Publication Data
Davies, Jacqueline.
Where the ground meets the sky / Jacqueline Davies.
p.   cm.
Summary: During World War II, a twelve-year-old girl is uprooted from her quiet,
East coast life and moved to a secluded army post in the New Mexico desert
where her father and other scientists are working on a top secret project.
ISBN 0-7614-5105-6
[1. Interpersonal relations—Fiction. 2. Manhattan Project (U.S.)—Fiction. 3. Atomic
bomb—Fiction. 4. Schools—Fiction. 5.Scientists—Fiction. 6. World War, 1939-
1945—United States—Fiction. 7..Los Alamos (N.M.)—Fiction.] I. Title.
PZ7.D2839 Wh 2002   [Fic]—dc21   2001032519

Goodnight, Irene, reprinted on page 182 by permission. *Goodnight, Irene*, words
and music by Huddie Ledbetter and John A. Lomax; TRO © 1936 (Renewed)
1950 (Renewed) Ludlow Music, Inc., New York NY.
Excerpts from *New York Times* articles dated August 6, 1943 reprinted on pages
75, 76, and 78, by permission of the *New York Times*.
Excerpt of an interview with Herbert York on page 223 was reprinted by
permission. The complete interview is included in *Atomic Fragments: A
Daughter's Questions*, by Mary Palevsky, University of California Press, 2000.

The text of this book is set in 12 point Sabon.
Book design by Constance Ftera
Printed in the United States of America
First edition
5 6 4

For John, of course

1

A Bomb Drops on Me

I dropped like a rock onto the second porch step, a little ways away from my parents, and tried hard to remember why I had wanted to come here. Something about starting over. Something about a clean slate. Something about the romance of war work. Something about mystery and intrigue, which there'd never been any of in my life. But let me tell you, looking around, I just couldn't get that feeling back. It was like mercury, gone at a touch.

My brain felt fuzzy from the days of travel. And I was pretty sure I'd left my stomach behind on the bus ride up the Hill. I couldn't think what to do, but sitting still made me want to scream. So I started to scrape my shoes.

They were a brand new pair of tan-and-white saddle shoes. I'd been so happy to buy them, back in Montclair, before we started our trip. It was 1944, and the war was going full tilt, so "doing without" was a way of life. But those shoes—I loved them the minute I saw them. They were just *right*, the kind of shoes that all the popular girls wore. And Mom had said yes. She was so distracted with closing up the house and hiding the truth about where we were going and canceling our milk delivery and finding someone to water her roses. She had said yes.

Now they were covered with mud—thick, oozing mud the color of half-dried blood. I scraped off as much as I could, then rolled down my bobby socks to hide the splatters that spotted them too.

My *parents*, meanwhile, were up to their ankles in it. They didn't care. They were holding hands and laughing, waiting for some guy from Housing to show up with the key. I hadn't seen my mom laugh like that for a month, not since my Dad disappeared that night.

Okay, he didn't really disappear, but I woke up one morning and he was gone and my Mom explained that he had left on a business trip. An *extended* business trip. Something having to do with the war, but she couldn't say what.

Now, you tell me. What would *you* think if your mom told you that your brainy scientist dad was gone— *poof!*—gone in the middle of the night to help win the war? Maybe you'd think your parents were splitting up? But that thought didn't even cross my mind. My parents are completely over the moon about each other. You've never seen grownups act the way they do. It's incredibly embarrassing. They met when they were *six years old* and fell in love when they were just teenagers. It's not a normal story. Nothing about my family is normal.

So it didn't even occur to me that my folks were splitting up. And they weren't. And here we were. But where was here?

As far as I could tell, this place didn't even have a

name. Everybody called it the Hill. Which is what it was—a giant hill somewhere in New Mexico with its head chopped off flat. The whole, flat top of the hill was surrounded by a chain-link fence with three runs of barbed wire circling the top. There was a gate with a wooden guardhouse, and that's where the bus that brought us here stopped. We all had to show our passes to get in. There were soldiers in the guardhouse and soldiers patrolling the fence. Besides me and Mom, everyone else on the bus was a soldier. The Hill was crawling with them. But I'd seen a few regular people, too. A woman hanging out laundry on a line, and another one with a baby on her hip. And I saw some Indian women with woven blankets over their shoulders standing together, talking. No men. No kids my age.

I finished scraping my left shoe on the bottom step, so I scooched up one to scrape my right shoe on the next step. The stairs were new and wooden and full of splinters. No one had bothered to sand or paint them. They ran up the outside of the two-story wooden house, connecting the bottom porch (ours) with the top porch (someone else's). There were rows and rows of these ugly houses, as far as I could see. Ugly, ugly, ugly. I suddenly thought of our house in Montclair—neat brick with sharply peaked gables, white linen curtains in the front windows, and the elm tree in front that I loved. Oh, I missed it! For the first time since leaving home, I missed what we had left behind.

I looked down at my shoes and felt like a cat was clawing the inside of my throat. I hadn't cried since I was two, and I wasn't going to start now. Crying is pointless, as far as I can tell. It won't put meat on the table or sweep the kitchen floor, is what my Nebraska granny would say. But what else could I do? I'd already scraped clean my shoes. What else was I supposed to do in this strange place?

Suddenly, I felt something land on my head and then heard it fall to the ground. It was a pinecone. I looked up. There wasn't a tree anywhere nearby. Then something else fell on my head and rolled onto the step. It was a crumpled-up piece of paper. I unballed the paper.

There was a single word written on it: "Hi!"

I looked up. And that's when I saw Eleanor.

2

Twins

Now that she'd gotten my attention, Eleanor started waving her arms like crazy to get me to climb the stairs up to the porch where she stood. She acted like she was a soldier trapped behind enemy lines and the Germans were closing in fast. By the look on her face, you'd have thought it was a matter of life or death.

"This is a crazy person," I thought. "I am *not* going up there."

But she wouldn't stop waving. So I turned to my parents to get some help, but they were standing in that sappy way they have, their heads bent together like two flowers reaching to the same sun. Useless.

So I climbed the stairs.

When I reached the top, Eleanor was waiting. She was at least a foot taller than me and pretty. I mean, really *pretty*. What I'm saying is, she definitely could have been on a magazine cover. But she was wearing blue jeans and cowboy boots! Like Roy Rogers! I'd never seen a girl dressed like that in my whole life. I couldn't believe her mother let her wear those clothes. I was so surprised, I couldn't say anything. She didn't say anything either. She just grabbed my arm and pulled me inside.

"Can you do this?" she asked, and then flipped herself over into a handstand and walked halfway across the living room.

"No," I answered. Immediately I felt like a goon. Why couldn't I do a handstand? I was sure every other twelve-year-old in America could do one. But that's just *one* of the problems of being the only kid of two very intelligent people. They teach you all about astronomy and philosophy and quantum theory and existentialism—which is all very interesting, really, it is—but they never show you how to ride a bike or jump rope or blow bubble gum or any of the really important stuff. Normal stuff. What I mean is the stuff you need to know to get through the day.

I started backing up, heading for the door. Then I thought of something else. "I can wiggle my ears," I said, and I began to wiggle.

"That's extremely neat," said the girl. "Ex-*treme*-ly. Can you teach me how?"

"I don't think so," I said. "It's genetic."

Eleanor's face became a big question mark.

"An ability or trait that's passed down from one generation to the next," I explained. "In other words, you have to be born with the ability. Or else you'll never be able to do it."

Eleanor gave me a long stare. "You're smart, aren't you?"

I hated myself. Here I was, in this strange place for less than an hour, and already I'd blown it. So much for starting over. So much for a clean slate. Why did I have to be smart like my dad? Why couldn't I just keep my mouth shut and learn to do handstands and chew bubble gum and say the kinds of things that make kids want to be your friend?

Eleanor was still looking at me, waiting for an answer.

"Not really," I mumbled. I figured that was it. She was pretty. I was smart. Those kinds of things never work out.

"Smart's okay," she said. "Especially around here. I used to be the smartest kid in my class back home. But *here*? Let me tell you, there are some *really* smart cookies in this town. Trust me. I know what I'm talking about."

"How long have you been here?" I asked.

"Almost a year. My parents and me were the first family to arrive."

I bit my tongue to keep "my parents and *I*" from popping out of my mouth. If this girl was willing to overlook the fact that I was smart, I was willing to overlook a little bad grammar.

"Still, I bet if I practice long enough," said Eleanor, and she trailed down the hallway straining her face, trying to make her ears wiggle.

I didn't know what to do. Was I supposed to follow her? Shouldn't I tell my parents where I was? They might be worried. On top of everything else, I still didn't know this girl's name. We hadn't really been introduced. And for all I knew, she was a lunatic.

This was *not* how things were done back in Montclair.

A minute later, she came back out of her bedroom,

turning a perfect cartwheel down the hall. "Well, aren't you coming?" she asked, a little annoyed.

"Oh, sure," I answered. "Just let me tell my folks." I figured I'd run downstairs and make an excuse for why I couldn't come back up. I mean, this girl was *bizarre*.

"Wait a sec!" she said, running past me. "Let's drop something on them first!"

Before I could say anything, she started pulling ammunition out of her pockets: another pinecone, a few small pebbles, and some more wads of paper. She handed one of the wads to me. "On the count of three, then duck!"

She ran out onto the porch and whispered, very dramatically, "One, two, three!" She lobbed the pinecone in the direction of my parents. Then she pulled me to the ground as if a grenade were about to go off. I still held on to the wad of paper in my hand. Eleanor pointed politely to it. "You were supposed to throw it," she whispered, as if I hadn't understood.

Suddenly my parent's conversation stopped. Then we heard my mom say, "Is it starting to rain again?"

Eleanor popped up like a cork out of a bottle. I followed slowly, hoping the look on my face made it clear that I had *nothing* to do with the whole thing.

"Hello! Hello!" shouted Eleanor. "I'm supposed to be in school, but Mom said I could skip so someone would be here to welcome you! My name is Eleanor. How do you do!"

"Very well, thank you, Eleanor," replied my mother. "And how are you?"

"Terrific! We've been waiting for you to show up for-*e*-ver. We thought you would come two weeks ago, but then we heard that Hazel had a piano recital." How did she know my name? How did she know I played the piano? "Then we thought you would come last week, but we heard that you made a mistake with the movers and gave them the wrong date, and so you couldn't come until this week, and now *here you are*!" Eleanor spread her arms out wide as though she thought she were personally responsible for our arrival.

My mom gave my dad her one-eyebrow-raised look. She said, "I guess it's a small town."

"You have no idea," said my dad.

"Can Hazel come and play at my house for awhile?" asked Eleanor. Now I definitely wanted to make an escape. This girl was like a chemical reaction out of control. Anything could happen! I stared at my mom with a look that said: *This girl is a maniac. Rescue me, please!*

But my mom didn't catch my expression. Or did she?

"Your mother's not home?" asked my mom.

"She's at work, with dad. All the moms on the Hill work. Except the ones with little babies. And the foreign ones. They don't want the foreign moms working in the Tech Area. *National security*," she said in a dramatic whisper. "We'll be fine!" she crowed. "I'm twelve, just like Hazel. Practically grown up!" She started to pull on my arm. Over my shoulder I caught a glimpse of my mother's face—smiling. I could tell she liked Eleanor. I was doomed.

I followed the crazy girl into her apartment.

"Do you want to change into a pair of blue jeans?" she asked, looking at my mud-splashed socks and wrinkled skirt. All the pleats in my skirt had gone kerflooey. I was a mess.

"I don't think my mother packed any blue jeans," I said.

"You can borrow a pair of mine. We'll just tie 'em with a belt and roll up the cuffs." Eleanor started to lead me into her bedroom.

What I hadn't told her (although I hadn't exactly lied) was that I didn't even own a pair of blue jeans. What kind of girl wears blue jeans? In Montclair, the answer was none.

"Here," she said, handing me a pair of pants from her dresser. "Try these. I've got some bridle rope that will hold them up." She began rummaging in a trunk in her closet.

I felt shy about taking off my skirt in front of her. I'd only known her for a few minutes. And besides, I had really skinny legs.

"Maybe I should just stick to my skirt," I said. "I wouldn't want to get your clothes dirty." I held onto the blue jeans. They felt stiff, more like cardboard than cloth. What would it feel like to wear pants? Part of me wanted to put them on. But it was too strange. Like wearing a costume when you're not at a Halloween party.

"Don't be ridiculous. You can't do anything in a skirt around here. Trust me. I know what I'm talking about."

Eleanor found the rope and had me double-knotted into her blue jeans in no time.

Standing side by side, we looked at ourselves in the mirror. We were like Dr. Jekyll and Mr. Hyde. Well, no, that's *hyperbole*, as my dad would say. He's a real stickler for the truth, and so is my mom. But what I mean is, we could not have looked more different.

Eleanor was tall and strong and had beautiful white skin, just like the movie stars. And her hair! She had the most beautiful, long, black hair I've ever seen, all waves and curls, pulled back with a pretty ribbon.

And me? Well, I was short—a runt, really—and thin like a twig. My skin was dark olive, like my mother's, which I did *not* find glamorous, despite what my mom said. My hair was dull and brown and straight as a stick— which is why I kept it braided and out of the way. I had brown eyes, a straight nose, and a smallish mouth. Okay. Nothing you'd see on the cover of a magazine, but okay.

Looking in the mirror, I couldn't help noticing how different Eleanor and I were. And how much, well . . . *better* she was, in just about every way that I could see. It made me feel sort of jealous and sad and kind of sorry for myself.

Eleanor, on the other hand, looked at our reflections with obvious satisfaction.

"Twins!" she declared, and she threw her arms around me like she just couldn't not.

3

Tested

The very first thing I did when I opened my eyes the next morning was check the clothesline outside my window. Eleanor and I had rigged up a loop of line that ran around two nails between her bedroom window and mine. You see, Eleanor's family's apartment was identical to our apartment. I mean, exactly. Same living room, same hallway, same bathroom, same bedroom, same couch, same kitchen table, same everything. And Eleanor's bedroom was directly over my bedroom, which made the clothesline a very practical way to communicate. There were no telephones on the Hill, and sometimes you just didn't want your parents hearing what you had to holler to your best friend.

Sure enough, there was a square of white paper clothespinned to the line outside my window. I snatched it and read Eleanor's loopy letters: "Don't wake me up in the morning. I need my beauty rest. I'll knock for you at O-800 hours. (That's military talk for eight o'clock.) Secret Agent Z." Eleanor was Secret Agent Z. I was Secret Agent Y. We'd decided that last night.

Eight o'clock! That was almost an hour away. What was I going to do until then? I got dressed and combed and braided my hair. In the kitchen, my mother was unpacking some boxes of dishes we had brought with us from home.

"What would you like for breakfast?" she asked. "I can offer you cornflakes with no milk, cornflakes with no milk, or cornflakes with no milk."

"What's wrong with the icebox?" I asked. The icebox door was wide open, and there was a very strange smell coming from it.

"Power outage," replied Mom. "Apparently they happen on a daily basis. Also . . . " She turned the water spigot with a great flourish. A trickle of water leaked out. "No running water. The General wants us to take water conservation seriously, so he's cut off our supply for a few hours."

"The General doesn't live on the Hill, does he?" I asked.

"Oh, no!" said my mom. "The General lives in Washington, D.C., a city where electricity and running water are just a part of everyday life. In fact, I'm told the General flushes his toilet whenever he likes. Unlike those of us on the Hill who have been told to flush just twice a day. Now what would you like for breakfast?"

"I'll have cornflakes, but could you hold the milk?"

"Cornflakes in the Sahara, coming up!" She laughed, but she looked tired.

After breakfast—we couldn't even wash the dishes, we just sort of wiped them clean—Eleanor appeared. She knocked, but then walked in without waiting for an invitation.

"Ready for school?" she asked standing at the door.

"Hazel's going to help me unpack," said my mom. "And tomorrow I thought we'd explore the town a bit. But you can walk together on Monday. Show her the way. That will be nice."

I looked at Eleanor. She looked at me.

"Unless," said my mom, catching our looks. "Unless, of course, you want to go to school, Hazel?"

Cripes. This was weird. I could tell my mom wanted me to stay. At home, we did a lot of things together. Shopping and errands and jigsaw puzzles and going to the movies. It would be fun, unpacking together and settling into the new apartment. Who would want to do that alone?

But Eleanor was tapping her foot and shifting her stack of books from one hip to the other. She looked at me, raised her eyebrows, and nodded her head toward the door. I had to choose?

"Of course," said my mom. "Of course. Go with Eleanor. It will be fun meeting your schoolmates and your new teacher. I have your enrollment card right here." She handed me a stiff piece of paper with an official stamp on it. "Would you like me to walk with you?"

But before I could answer, Eleanor said, "We'll be fine! The walk's a cinch. A piece of cake! 'Bye!" Eleanor pulled me out the door, and we ran the six short blocks holding hands.

The school was the oddest thing: flat like a pancake, made out of wood, and painted pea green. It sat in a sort of gully so that you could hardly even see it as you walked up. And behind it, like puppet scenery, was a wall of pine trees and the most incredible mountains. Towering, purple mountains, like giant bears asleep.

"Those are the Jemez," said Eleanor. She pulled me impatiently past knots of girls skipping rope and boys tossing footballs or hanging around with their hands in their pockets. "Come on," she urged.

She led me inside and right up to the sixth-grade teacher's desk.

"This," said Eleanor, taking a step away, "is Hazel Moore."

The teacher, Miss Burrows, was pretty and young. Her silky hair was cut in a bob that curled under in just the right places, and her lipstick was the color of cherries. It was clear that Eleanor wanted to impress her. I stood up tall, which isn't easy for a runt like me, and hoped I looked impressive; I didn't want to let Eleanor down.

Miss Burrows looked over my card and smiled at me. "It's nice to have you with us, Hazel," she said. "You can start the morning with us, and then I'll have Eleanor take you to the principal's office for your entrance exam. Eleanor, why don't you show Hazel to the sixth-grade table."

"What exam?" I hissed as Eleanor led me to a long wooden picnic table by the windows.

"It's a cinch," she said. "And it doesn't even count. All the kids had to take it." She pointed to another picnic table closer to the door. "That's where the fifth-graders sit. We have to share teachers here."

"What's the stage for?" I asked, looking at a little raised platform on one side of the room.

"We put on plays and perform songs and recite poetry. This is the *best* school. Trust me. I know what I'm talking about."

Miss Burrows walked out of the room, and Eleanor pulled me to my feet. "Look here. Quick!" She ran over to the cupboards that lined one wall and opened a cupboard door and then another and another. Inside were stacks of paper and jars of pencils and pots of paint and piles of books. I couldn't believe it. Ever since the war had started, paper was like gold. And paint—we hadn't had any at our school for over a year. Pencils were hoarded like money. I'd been using the same stub of a pencil for most of sixth grade.

"This school has everything," said Eleanor proudly. Just then the bell rang, and we ran back to the table. Within a minute, both picnic tables were crowded with a mixed-up bunch of kids, about twenty in all. Most of them looked Mexican, and had names like Bences and Severo and Maria. Others of them had white, white skin and spoke with heavy accents—Italian and Russian and Polish. One of the fifth-grade girls was Hungarian and didn't speak much English at all. There was even an Indian boy, with two long, black braids—longer than mine! Eleanor quickly introduced me to Gemma, a dark-haired girl with a gap between her teeth. She had a heavy Italian accent. When she said hello to me, she said, "'Ello, 'Azel."

Miss Burrows called the class to order with a clap of

her hands. We all stood and faced a large American flag hanging in one corner. With our hands over our hearts, we recited the Pledge of Allegiance. Then we sang "My Country 'Tis of Thee." It felt good to do something familiar in this strange place.

Miss Burrows made me stand while she introduced me to the class. Then she sent me off, with Eleanor as my escort, to the principal's office. Eleanor was right: The test was a cinch. But it took almost two hours to finish because it was timed. I didn't give it another thought until the next day when Miss Burrows sent me home with a note. The note asked my mother to come to school that afternoon for a teacher conference.

"Did she have a conference with *your* mother?" I asked Eleanor on the way home.

"Nope. My mom doesn't have time for conferences. She's always at work."

"Maybe I should tell Miss Burrows that my mom works," I said.

"Hazel!" laughed Eleanor. "This is the Hill. You can't get away with a lie like that. Everybody knows every-thing about everybody else. Trust me. I know what I'm talking about. By the way," she added. "When *is* your mom going to start work?"

"We've only been here three days!" I said.

"Never too soon to help win the war," she answered.

I gave the note to my mother. She brushed her hair, and we were out the door.

"I don't think she meant for me to tag along," I said.

"The note says she wants to talk to *you*." I was dying to ditch out. Conferences with teachers are never good news.

"Come," said my mother, her long legs eating up the six blocks between our apartment and the school.

I could tell Miss Burrows was surprised when we walked in together. She had this little silk scarf twisted around her tiny neck, and she kept tugging at it the whole time we were there. She shook my mother's hand, then suggested I walk down the hall to look at the library.

"Oh, I think she'll learn more if she stays here with us," said my mom.

"But I meant for this to be a parent/teacher conference, Mrs. Moore. So that we could talk freely, the two of us," said Miss Burrows.

"Wonderful! I'm always so pleased when Hazel has the chance to hear adults talk freely," said my mom. "It doesn't happen very often, you know."

If Miss Burrows was flustered, she didn't show it. She sat down and invited us to do the same.

That's when I saw my test booklet on Miss Burrows' desk. I was starting to figure out where we were headed.

"I'm sure you're aware that Hazel is a very bright girl," began Miss Burrows. "I just don't know if you realize how extremely bright she is. Her IQ score ranks her at the very, very top *nationwide*. Within the school, she out-ranks all the students, and that includes the high school students. I would guess her IQ is as high as many of the men on the Hill. And that's saying quite a lot."

Boom. Boom. My cheeks burned red. My temples

began to pulse. Always the same, no matter where I went. The smart one. The freak.

"I'm sure you understand why we can't place her in the sixth grade. She would be completely out of her element. In fact, I can't imagine her in the seventh grade, either. I think we should start her out with the eighth-graders, and see where she goes from there."

My face was flaming with shame. Why not just brand me on the forehead—a great big G for Goon. Everybody would know. I would be the puniest eighth-grader on the Hill. I could hear the teasing now. None of the eighth-graders would be my friend. None of the sixth-graders would be my friend. I would be alone.

"No, thank you, Miss Burrows," said my mom. "We'll keep Hazel in the sixth grade."

Miss Burrows stared at my mom with her mouth wide open, like a trout feeding at sunset. I tried not to look down her throat.

"That's really not an option," stammered Miss Burrows. "She wouldn't learn a thing in the sixth-grade class."

"There's a lot to learn in this world, don't you agree Miss Burrows? I'm sure Hazel will find some way to exercise her brain. She always has."

"No, Mrs. Moore, I'm afraid you don't understand. . ."

"Every year, it's the same. Since she entered kindergarten reading Mark Twain. Everybody tells me to push her forward. Skip this year. Skip that year. Grow up faster. No, Miss Burrows. Hazel's brain will advance very well on its own. I'm more concerned about the rest of her catching up."

"I have nothing to teach her," said Miss Burrows.

"You'll find something. And if you don't, she will. She's very good at that."

"But . . ."

"Here's an idea. Let's ask Hazel. After all, she's the smartest one in this room." My mom turned to me. "Hazel, do you want to be in the eighth grade this year?"

"No," I croaked.

"Do you want to be in the sixth grade, with Eleanor, with other kids your own age?"

"Yes," I answered, like I was some idiot who only spoke in one-syllable words.

My mom shook hands enthusiastically with Miss Burrows. "It's going to be a wonderful year, I can tell," she said. "I just have a feeling about it."

Miss Burrows was still too flabbergasted to say anything more than "It was lovely to meet you."

Outside, I grabbed my mom's hand. "Hold on a minute," I said. "You never told me that my teachers in Montclair wanted me to skip any grades. How come?"

"Well," answered my mom, holding my hand and swinging it while we walked. "I didn't want you to think you were too different from all the other kids, because sometimes kids think different is bad. On the other hand, I didn't want you to think you were too special, you know, something extraordinary and better than all the other kids. Remember Hazel, you are blessed with intelligence, which is a wonderful thing. But that doesn't make you more valuable than any other person walking on this earth. We all count the same."

You know, I always say my dad is the smart one in the family. But sometimes my mom wins, hands down.

4

Saying No

"I'm surprised you and Eleanor haven't worn out the steps between our apartments," said my mom.

"Now *that's* hyperbole," I said. I was in a rush, eating my cereal as fast as I could. It was Saturday morning, no school, and Eleanor had a plan. Last night, she had run a note down the clothesline saying to meet upstairs at O-800 hours. It was already ten minutes past. Why did my mom always make me eat every single bite of my breakfast? Eleanor's mom wasn't even around for breakfast most mornings.

"I'm not so sure," she said, "what with the way everything is built around here. Houses put up in a day. Huts rolled in on trailers—Slow down! Don't shovel your food like that!—Every time I walk on those stairs, I wonder if they're going to collapse right under me. And the whole town is a fire trap."

She was rattling the doors on Black Beauty, the enormous iron stove that burned wood and took up half the kitchen. Every day since we'd moved in, my mom had been trying to get that stove to work. But the one time she managed to get the fire to catch, she ended up with a kitchen full of black smoke and a plate full of burned food.

"That's it! You win!" she yelled at the stove. "Today,

I'm going over to Housing and filling out a req for a hot plate and an electric roaster. You," she said, banging a stove lid, "are now a planter!"

There was a knocking sound—as if the stove were making some sort of answer! We were both so surprised, it took us a second to figure out what it was—someone at the front door.

When my mom opened the front door, a man in an army uniform stood there. He whipped off his hat and made a ducking bow with his head. There was nothing unusual about that. Most of the folks on the Hill dressed in some sort of uniform. My mom invited him in.

"Hazel," she said. "Since you're finished with your breakfast, why don't you go on up to Eleanor's?"

I had my spoon in my mouth and at least half a bowl of cereal in front of me. Finished? TGTBT, I thought to myself—one of Eleanor's favorite phrases: too good to be true. I dropped the spoon in my bowl, ran out the door, and took the stairs two at a time.

What was it that made me turn back? I can't honestly say. An intuition, like my mom gets? If so, it was the first and last of my life. But whatever the reason, I crept back down the stairs and listened outside the screen door.

I heard the army man say, "That's a lovely young girl you've got there."

"The light of my life," my mom answered.

"Ma'am. I'm sorry to bother you first thing in the morning, and on a Saturday, too. But the war doesn't wait for business hours. I'm here to ask you to fill out a questionnaire listing your job skills and training so that we can find a suitable position for you as soon as possible. That would include bookkeeping, typing, or secretarial skills. As you know, it's vital that every wife on the Hill does her part for the war effort. And since you don't have little ones at home—"

"I'm sorry, Sergeant," my mother said. I jumped at her interruption. My mom never interrupts. "But I won't be working here on the Hill."

"Rest assured, Ma'am, we will provide all the domestic help you require. Cleaning service for your apartment, after-school supervision for your daughter. All compliments of the United States Army. I'm sure that will allow you time to do your share."

"It isn't a question of time. I will not be working here on the Hill."

"Mrs. Moore." The Sergeant spoke slowly, as if he were talking to a child. "Are you aware of the significance of the work being done here? Do you realize that the efforts of the men and women at this site could end the war? Could save thousands of American lives?"

"I am fully aware of the work being done here. But, as I said, I will not contribute to the effort."

I heard the Sergeant put the cap on his pen with a click.

"My sincerest apologies for wasting your time, Ma'am. I will certainly include all that you have said in my report. Good day."

I hid under the stairs. After the army man clomped by, I sat quietly, trying to puzzle it out. At home, my mom had done more than her fair share to win the war. She had led newspaper drives and scrap drives and war stamp drives. She'd had the best victory garden in the whole neighborhood. And she had even started a group to help the gold-star mothers in our town.

I remember the first time I saw a gold-star banner in our neighborhood. It was just months after the war began. By then, I was used to seeing the pretty blue-star banners in the windows of houses on our street, each one made out of cloth, with a single blue star sitting on a field of white satin surrounded by a red felt border. Each blue star stood for a son who was fighting overseas. But that morning I noticed that Mrs. Jorvack's house had two blue-star banners and one banner with a gold star.

"Why is it gold?" I asked. The blue was so much prettier.

"Mrs. Jorvack's youngest son was killed in the Philippines. That's what the gold star means. The loss of a life. The grief of a mother."

That afternoon, my mom organized a group of mothers to help whenever someone in the neighborhood lost a son. They made meals and did the housekeeping and took care of any little kids in the house. While the mother grieved.

So how come my mom didn't want to help with the war effort on the Hill? It was unpatriotic.

I waited under the porch stairs until my legs cramped up. Then I crawled out and walked back into our apartment.

"Forgot something in my room," I announced.

My mom was staring out the window. The Sangre de

Cristo mountains lay in morning shadow. I walked over to where she stood, then slipped my head under one of her arms. We both looked at the mountains for a minute, and then she whispered, "What have I done?"

I'm not sure what she meant. What have I done by saying no to the Sergeant? What have I done by coming here? Maybe she meant both.

I didn't know the question, and I sure didn't know the answer, so I didn't say anything.

"Will you be home for lunch?" asked my mom, turning toward the kitchen. She cleared away my cereal bowl and rinsed it in the sink.

"Sure," I said. I ran to the door, then stopped. "What are *you* going to do today?" I asked.

"Are you kidding?" she asked. "I have a list a mile long. Laundry, PX, not to mention that trip to Housing. Plus I promised to help Mrs. Embley with something called the Mesa Club. It's a funny place, the Hill. In the middle of nowhere, but you can't step outside your door without tripping over a club or a committee. See you at lunch, then."

I ducked out the door and tore up the stairs.

5

Reconnaissance

"Good morning, Mrs. Talbot," I said, as I walked into Eleanor's apartment. "How are you?"

"Late!" she answered, pulling on her gloves and tacking a hat to her head. "I should have been at the Tech Area half an hour ago. Eleanor! Eleanor!"

No answer. Music blared from down the hall.

"Go right in, dear," said Mrs. Talbot, stuffing food into a paper bag. I walked down the hall and into Eleanor's room.

Eleanor was pulling on her blue jeans and scooping her hair into a ponytail, dancing to Bing Crosby and the Andrews Sisters singing "Hot Time in the Town of Berlin." There was a radio station on the Hill with a GI who spun the records. He did a pretty okay job.

"Hi there," she mumbled with her comb in her mouth. "Did you get my note this morning?"

"I got your note last night, but there wasn't anything on the line this morning. I checked."

Eleanor's right eyebrow shot up. She stuck her head out the window and looked down. "Oh. It fell on the ground." Down below in the dirt, I spotted a white square of paper.

"What does it say?" I asked.

Mrs. Talbot's voice hollered from the living room. "Eleanor! Don't forget to feed Dinah!" We heard the front door slam shut.

Dinah was Eleanor's cat, but I'd never even seen her. She spent all day outside, and sometimes she didn't even come home at night. She was a roamer, sort of like the kids on the Hill, except that we always came home for meals.

"So, the note . . . ?" I asked.

Eleanor grabbed me by the shoulders and whispered in her most dramatic voice, "The enemy is everywhere. We must be prepared! In case of a surprise attack in the middle of the night, I've got an escape plan." She grabbed a knotted rope from under her bed and threw it out the window. One end of the rope was tied to the bed. Without even a how-do-you-do, she swung her legs over the windowsill and disappeared.

I looked at the bed. I looked at the rope. If it was strong enough to hold Eleanor, it was strong enough to hold me. But what about *my* strength? I could just imagine my skinny arms giving out halfway down. *Then* where would I be?

But I didn't have a choice. I'd never had a friend like Eleanor. But having a friend like her came with a cost—which on this particular day included falling to my death.

I grabbed hold of the rope and swung my legs over the edge of the sill. The rope burned my hands, but I did a good job of hanging on. I didn't slip at all. Slowly I climbed down, like an inchworm on a blade of grass, until I heard Eleanor whisper, "Jump!" And I did.

My feet landed in an inch of mud that slopped over the tops of my sneakers and squished inside my shoes.

That's when we saw *the enemy*—two MPs on horse-back—sneaking up behind us.

"Keep low!" hissed Eleanor. "Circle left. I'll circle right. Meet me on top of High Rock. If you get caught, YOU KNOW NOTHING!" And she was gone.

Running in mud is difficult. Running quietly in mud is impossible. I tried to stay low to the ground, but the mud kept sucking me in. The MPs were patrolling the fence. That was one of their jobs, to make sure no one got in—or out. That's what made them the enemy. Sometimes we pretended they were the Nazis. Or the Japanese. Or the Italian Fascists. But mostly, we just called them the enemy. They wore uniforms and helmets and rode as if they had broomsticks up their backs. I could see their guns, shining in their holsters.

I ran straight for the fence. I could hear the horses off to my left, but I didn't dare look in that direction. It only took me a couple of minutes to get to the part of the fence that had a hole dug under it.

The very first rule I learned on the Hill was that kids were *not* allowed to tunnel under the fence. The army was very clear about that. Of course, that's what made it so much fun. On my first day, Eleanor had shown me how to worm my way under. By my third day, I was an old pro.

And there were *always* holes under the fence. The

problem was the holes kept moving. That's because us kids kept digging them and the MPs kept filling them in. So sometimes, you'd go looking for a hole and it would be gone. It was practically a full-time job for us kids, keeping up on where the holes were.

Lucky for me, the hole I was looking for was still there, but it had about two inches of rainwater in it. Yuck. I covered my nose and mouth and scrambled under the fence. When I reached the other side, sopping wet, I heard one MP say to the other, "Gopher at two o'clock."

My heart started thumping, and I *ran*! I ran for my life. I crashed through the woods, expecting to hear the pounding of hooves as the MPs closed in on me. What would they do to me if they caught me? Jail, most likely, but there was no jail on the Hill. Would they send me to Santa Fe? Back east to Montclair? As these thoughts raced though my brain, I saw High Rock up ahead. I made straight for it and grabbed Eleanor's outstretched hand. We scrambled to the top and lay flat like lizards, peering in all directions.

All was quiet.

No one came after us.

"I can't believe we made it," whispered Eleanor. "TGTBT."

I was breathing so hard, I couldn't answer.

All of a sudden, Eleanor laughed. She let out this burst of laughter that echoed all the way to the Jemez Mountains and back again. When my heart stopped pounding in my ears, I laughed too.

We were both soaking wet and covered in mud. We took off our shoes and scooped out as much mud as we could. Then we stretched out on the rock. The whole canyon lay below us. The whole day lay ahead. In twenty minutes our clothes would be dry. Eleanor took an apple out of her pocket and offered me the first bite. Then she took a great big bite herself.

With her mouth full of apple, she asked, "What do you want to do now?"

6

Bits and Pieces

I think Miss Burrows was afraid of me in the beginning. She got this worried expression on her face whenever she looked my way. Her eyebrows dipped down on the outsides, like I was a shocking sight.

Maybe I should have explained it to her. Maybe I should have told her I was working undercover. Maybe I should have told her what my life had been like back in Montclair, being the smart one every year. The hissing of "teacher's pet" as I walked down the row of desks to my seat after writing on the blackboard. Then she would have understood why I never raised my hand and why I answered "I don't know" every time she called on me.

Well I didn't explain it to her. Let her figure it out for herself.

One day, Miss Burrows clapped her hands at the end of recitation and said, "Sixth grade, divide for math." It sounded like a joke, but I didn't get it.

The class did, though. It divided, just like Miss Burrows said. Eleanor, Gemma, and Walter slid their books and papers down to one end of the picnic table, and Dimas, Maria, Bences, Anita, and Severo moved over to a separate table by the door. It didn't take me more than a second to figure out which group I belonged with. I slid down to the end with the other scientists' kids.

Miss Burrows was busy handing out flashcards to the Spanish kids. Multiplication and division. "Work in pairs," she told them.

"What's going on?" I asked Eleanor. "How come we split up?"

"The Spanish kids are way behind in math. They still don't know their times tables."

"Oh," I said. But how are they ever going to catch up, I wondered, if they don't sit with us during math lessons?

Miss Burrows returned to our table. "Fractions. Let's pick up where we left off last week." She turned to write on the chalkboard. Her white chalk flashed like a knife against the black of the board. She copied out a long list of fractions to be added. Most of the fractions had different denominators, and some of the fractions were negative numbers. Gemma, Walter, and Eleanor were busy copying the lists of fractions into their notebooks. I could do the addition in my head, so I wondered if I should bother to copy the fractions into my book.

While I was wondering, Miss Burrows turned from the board and noticed Severo, standing.

"Yes, Severo?"

"I'd like to do fractions today."

"You need to memorize your multiplication and division first."

"I have," he said politely. "I am ready for fractions."

"Severo, dear," said Miss Burrows kindly. "I plan to

introduce fractions to your group in a few weeks. I promise you will learn everything in your own time. For now, I need you to drill your times tables."

"I don't have a partner," said Severo.

Miss Burrows counted heads. "Oh, yes. Antonio is out sick today. Well . . ."

I raised my hand. "I could drill with him, Miss Burrows." The fraction work was a waste of time for me. I might as well do something useful.

She hesitated. "I suppose," she said. Then she gave me a sharp glance. "For today."

Eleanor smiled and crossed her eyes at me to let me know she thought I was nuts. But I walked over to the other table anyway to sit with the Spanish kids.

Severo *did* know his times tables. We whipped through the stack of flashcards in three minutes flat. He hardly even paid attention, he was so busy looking at the board where the fraction work was being done.

"Fractions are a cinch," I whispered, gathering the cards.

"For you, maybe," he said.

"For anyone. There's nothing to it. It's just about taking one thing and breaking it down into bits and pieces, then putting those pieces back together." I tore a page from my notebook. "I'll show you."

I folded the paper into four rectangles, then ripped the paper along the folds. "This is one piece of paper, but I've ripped it into four equal little pieces. Fractions tell us about pieces. The bottom number in a fraction is how many pieces you start with to make one whole piece of paper. So, for this piece of paper, the bottom number is four because I ripped the page into four pieces. Now, the top number is how many of the little pieces you're holding." I handed Severo one little piece of paper. "You've got one out of four pieces, so you have one-fourth." I wrote the fraction on another piece of paper. "Pretty easy, huh?"

"Yeah. I get that," he said.

"Now, look. You've got one-fourth. Here's another one-fourth." I handed him the second little piece of paper. "And here's another one-fourth." I handed him the third little piece of paper. "And here's another one-fourth." I handed him the last little piece of paper. "So if you taped all those little bits of paper together, how many big pieces of paper would you have?"

Severo spread the four pieces of paper on the table, lining up their torn edges.

"One," he said.

"Right. One-fourth plus one-fourth plus one-fourth plus one-fourth equals one." I shrugged. "That's fractions. Just bits and pieces that add up to one."

Severo smiled. "I get it." Then he looked at me out of the sides of his eyes. "How come you're so smart?" he asked.

"I'm not," I said. "I just know about fractions, that's all."

7

For the Duration

Every morning, my dad walked out the door at 7:00 to go to work. Saturdays, too. Sometimes, when I got up early enough, I walked with him. It was a short trip down the dirt road that went past dozens of apartment buildings just like ours. One left turn, loop around Ashley Pond, and there you were: at the guardhouse to the Tech Area. Dad would say hello to all the other men walking through the gate, give me a quick kiss, show his white security badge to the guard, and then disappear. My mom and I could never go in. We didn't have white security badges.

Whenever my dad walked through that gate, I felt like he was getting on a giant ship that was about to sail far away from us. Would he come back tonight? Tomorrow? Next week? I really wasn't sure.

Sometimes he came home for dinner and then went back to the Tech Area. Sometimes he stayed at work through dinner and returned late at night, after I was asleep. And sometimes he flopped on a cot in his lab and slept there all night. That was when we knew something was bothering him. Something at work. Something having to do with the gadget.

The gadget was the Big Mystery. The gadget was the

whole reason we were on the Hill. The gadget was what was going on in the Tech Area. And there was this unwritten rule on the Hill that you didn't ask about the gadget.

But I had to know. There was no way I was going to wait until the end of the war to find out. We had been on the Hill for a week, and I decided to just out and out ask. After all, like my parents always say: If I'm old enough to ask the question, I'm old enough to hear the answer. That's how I learned where babies come from long before any of my friends did. Which is a whole other can of worms, believe you me.

'Course, sometimes knowing too much gets you into trouble. Like the time I was six and I explained evolution to the kids in my neighborhood and Timmy Smith went home crying and told his parents that the Bible was just a story and not the true word of God. Or the time when I was four and I told Jane Wiley that everybody, absolutely everybody, would die someday, even her mom and dad, even her pet hamster.

Sometimes I find out more than I want to know.

But not that night. It was the first time Dad had been home for dinner in three nights, and my mom was *so* happy. I could tell because she put candles on the table and her favorite record on the phonograph—Lena Horne singing "Just One of Those Things." She had picked a big bunch of wildflowers that morning—irises and anemones and lupine—and she put them in a big coffee can in the middle of the table. Just like a party.

When we all sat down to eat, she made us hold hands in a circle and give thanks for us all being together. It was sort of like a prayer except that my mom isn't religious. Well, really she is religious. She just can't decide which religion to be religious with. She's tried the Top Ten: Christianity, Judaism, Buddhism, et cetera, et cetera. But, according to my mom, they all have failings. I could write a whole book on my mom's problems with religion.

For now, she's decided to be a Humanitarian Spiritualist. That's a religion she made up, and it has only one rule: With every action, with every word, ask yourself these questions: Who am I helping? Who am I hurting? It's not a bad religion, if you ask me. At least it isn't complicated like the rest of them.

Of course, I wasn't about to tell any of the other kids on the Hill that my mother was a Humanitarian Spiritualist. Not even Eleanor. She was a Lutheran! That's the kind of thing that gets you locked in the coat closet during recess. I know from experience.

Anyway, at dinner that night, my mom was in such a good mood and my dad was home for a change, so I thought it would be the perfect time to clear up the Big Mystery.

"Dad, can I please have some more potatoes?" We were having canned ham and mashed potatoes and limp, gray spinach. During the war, the vegetables were just terrible. All the farmers were off fighting in Europe and the Pacific.

"And there's something I'd really like to know. I know

it's a big secret, and all. But I'm twelve years old, so I think I'm old enough to know. So, could you tell me, what is the gadget?"

My dad looked at my mom and then reached for more potatoes himself.

"Where did you hear about the gadget?"

"Around. You know, I pay attention. Pick up things."

"You're an observant girl. Good. Observation is the most important skill that a scientist can develop. So, you've heard about the gadget. Is this what you and Eleanor talk about when you're roaming the canyons?"

"Not always. Not usually. Well, really, not ever. You always say when I have a question, go straight to the source. So I figured I should ask you."

Dad laughed. "Sorry to disappoint you, but I'm not the source. I'm just one of the drones. One puny scientist among giants."

Now, my Dad is *not* puny. And I don't just mean his size. My dad happens to be one of the world's leading atomic physicists. He has had several papers published in the *Journal of Physics*. And at Columbia—which is a *very good* university—he is a full professor, even though he's only thirty-two. That is *not* puny. That is huge.

"Well, if you're puny, then who are the giants on the Hill? Enrico Fermi?" I asked.

My father dropped his fork. My mother stood up from the table to refill the water pitcher.

"How do you know Fermi is here?" asked my dad.

"I saw him walking down the street."

"How did you recognize him? You've never met him before."

"You showed me his picture in the newspaper. A while ago. Remember? When he did that great experiment. Remember, when he caused a sustained nuclear reaction? You remember that, don't you? You were all excited and couldn't wait to explain the whole thing to me. How he made an atom of uranium absorb an extra neutron and that made the atom unstable so it divided in half. And that made more neutrons fly out of the two little atoms, and then those neutrons were absorbed by other atoms of uranium. And that kept going and going and going. Remember? You showed me how it happened with a bunch of grapes. You said it was the most exciting discovery of the century. And his picture was in the paper. And then I saw him walking down the street here."

My dad stared at me like he was noticing for the first time that I had a third eye in the middle of my forehead. My mom wasn't looking at me. She was looking at my dad. And I think I saw a tiny smile on her face.

"Not much gets by you, does it?" He pushed his chair back from the table as if he needed a little extra room.

He paused for a long time before continuing. "Well, let's begin at the beginning. First of all, Fermi *is* here. But you're not supposed to know that. If you're ever in Santa Fe or anywhere off the Hill and you have to mention his name, for God's sake, don't say Enrico Fermi. The G2 will be on us like ducks on a june bug. Off site, call him Mr. Henry Farmer. Can you remember that?"

"Sure. But why?"

"For the same reason I can't say the real name of this town."

"You mean it has a real name?" I asked. This was getting interesting.

"Of course it has a real name. The Hill is just a—a—a codename, like a nickname for the army."

"What's the real name?"

"I'm not allowed to say!"

"But *why*?"

"Because that's what the General wants. And whatever the General wants . . . ," began my father.

". . . the General gets!" we all shouted in a chorus.

The General was in charge of everything that happened on the Hill. When our drinking water got too muddy, the General decided whether or not to put in new pipes. When the grownups on the Hill wanted to start a town council, they had to get the General's okay. And when the moms got together to petition for a larger commissary that wouldn't always be running out of things like pork chops and chicken broth, it was the General who said, "Don't you know there's a war going on?" Eleanor told me that the General came to the Hill every month or so to check up on us. But I hadn't seen him yet.

Actually, there was one part of the Hill that the General *didn't* run—the Tech Area. Oppie was in charge there. Oppie's real name was J. Robert Oppenheimer, but everyone called him Oppie. It was a perfect name for him. He looked like some sort of funny marionette come to life.

He was tall and as thin as a stick—and all angles. Everywhere you looked on him, there was a sharp point. Dad said that Oppie was the smartest man he ever met.

"Does Edward Teller have a secret name?" I asked. "Or Hans Bethe?"

"Anna!" cried my dad, turning to my mom. "Have you been talking to her about these things?"

"Not one word," said my mother. "Honestly, she's hardly around long enough for me to say 'Good morning' or 'Good night.'"

I rushed to explain. "I saw Teller at Fuller Lodge when we had dinner there last week. And Bethe was in the PX on Saturday. Remember, I met them when there was that big conference at Columbia a few years ago. The one with all the physicists from all over the world. Mom and I met you for lunch, and you introduced us to Edward Teller and Hans Bethe. I remember, don't you?"

"Of course I remember, but you were only nine!"

I shrugged my shoulders. "I have a good memory."

"Anna, help me here."

"This is your pudding, Paul," said my mom. She was *definitely* smiling now.

My dad took off his glasses and laid them on the table. He rubbed his eyes the way he does when he's tired. It took him a long time to reposition them just so on his face.

"First of all, we are not to use the word 'physicist' while we are on the Hill. I know it seems silly, but that's the rule."

"I know. Eleanor already explained that to me. The

physicists are called 'fizzlers,' and the chemists are called 'stinkers.'"

My parents both burst out laughing. "Obviously, we should all be taking security lessons from Eleanor," said my dad. "Actually, you're supposed to call all the people here 'engineers.' The army thinks that's obscure enough. Is that understood?" I nodded my head. "Secondly, Teller and Bethe do *not* have secret names, as you say, but don't mention them when you're off the Hill either. Is *that* understood?"

"Yes, yes," I said. "But what are they doing here? What are they researching? And what is the gadget?"

My dad sighed. "We are researching the possible application of certain scientific discoveries that are not, as yet, fully understood. When we reach a more comprehensive understanding of the scientific phenomena surrounding these discoveries, we will be in a position to decide whether or not those discoveries have any bearing on the outcome of the war."

"You're not answering my question," I accused him. "You're being evasive. Why won't you tell me the truth? You *always* tell me the truth."

My dad looked helplessly at my mom. My mom held up her hands and said, "What can I say, Paul? The acorn doesn't fall far from the tree."

"Anna, please! A little help."

My mother sat down at the table and looked right at me. She has this way of fixing a person with her stare. It's like magic. You can't turn away. "Hazel. You know I'm not a scientist. I can't help explain the research your dad is doing here. But I can tell you this. Your father, like all the other men on the Hill, was asked to come here by the government of the United States. There is a war going on, and the government feels that the men on the Hill might be able to apply their special knowledge to speed the end of the war."

I wiggled in my chair impatiently, but my mother held me with her stare. I swear, it's magic.

"Your father came here out of a feeling of patriotism and a sense of duty to his country. And I respect and admire those impulses. But part of the agreement he made with the government is that he would not reveal anything having to do with the project. To anyone. Even you. I know that's hard to accept because we've never had any secrets in our family. You know how your dad and I feel about secrets. But this is an extraordinary case, and we are living in extraordinary times."

I had never thought about that before. That I was living in an extraordinary time. But my mom wasn't finished.

"And so, even though I object to . . . no, that isn't strong enough. How should I put this? I reject—yes, that's the word—I *reject* this place and what is going on here, I respect and admire your father for honoring his commitment and doing what he feels is right."

My father reached across the table and took my mother's hand.

"Thank you, Anna."

"I've missed you, Paul," said my mom. "I miss the way we used to talk in the evenings. I miss being a part of your life."

"I miss you, too. But this is so important. More important than anything I've ever done. Or ever will do. And it's only for the duration. When the war is over, we'll go back home. I promise. Everything will be just like it was."

"The other wives, they don't seem to mind as much. They keep busy. I've been keeping busy, too. But, it's just not enough."

"When the war is over. I promise. When the war is over, everything will be just like it was."

My father pulled my mother onto his lap, and they held on to each other as if they were the only survivors of a shipwreck.

Needless to say, I never again asked either one of them about the gadget. Case closed.

8

A Hill of Beans

The next morning, I didn't wait for Eleanor to knock on my door. I went upstairs and walked right in. Her parents were gone. I'd seen them leave. Eleanor usually slept until ten minutes before we had to leave for school. So I just let myself in and headed down the hall.

"Eleanor," I whispered outside her closed bedroom door.

"Come on in!" shouted Eleanor.

"What are you doing up?" I stopped short in the doorway. There was Eleanor, lying on her back on the floor. On her stomach was an orange and white cat.

I'm not much of a cat fan. Really, I can't stand them. They're so self-satisfied. They seem to think the world belongs to them. And all that purring! It's so subterranean. I'd much rather have a dog that barks when it's happy and growls when it's mad.

Like Timoshenko. Timoshenko was a Russian wolfhound that had once belonged to an MP. But the MP got transferred off the Hill, and when he left, he didn't take Timoshenko with him. So now Timoshenko belonged to the whole Hill. Everybody fed him. Everybody played with him. Everybody let him sleep on their porches or in their furnace rooms.

He was a smart dog, but he had this terrible habit of jumping up out of nowhere, stealing whatever you were holding in your hands, and running off with it. Once he even grabbed Oppie's briefcase and dashed off. You should have seen the MPs chase him all over the Hill. It's a bad habit. I admit that. But at least you always know where you stand with Timoshenko.

But cats are a different story. Cats never get right to the point. They're so secretive.

And *this* cat had green gunk in its eyes.

"What is that?" I said.

"Not what!" said Eleanor. "Who! This is Dinah. My best friend."

Well, what did that make me?

"I meant, what is that green slime oozing out of the cat's eyes. It's disgusting."

"Dinah has conjunctivitis. Isn't that so sad! We had to take her to Dr. Coles, and he gave us ointment for her eyes."

Doctor Coles was a people doctor, but everyone brought their pets to him, too. There were a lot of animals on the Hill—horses and cats and dogs, even some chickens and a parrot. Dr. Coles always started the exam with, "I'm no expert on (whatever animal he was looking at)." Still, there hadn't been an animal death on the Hill yet, so you had to figure that Doctor Coles knew something about something.

"Poor baby!" said Eleanor. "She's not allowed out. It's extr-*eme*-ly contagious!" Eleanor seemed to think this was thrilling news. She kissed Dinah right on the nose and crooned, "You are the best cat." *kiss* "And a brave cat."

kiss "And an adventurous cat." *kiss* "And you keep all my secrets." *kiss* "And I love you best." *kiss, kiss, kiss.*

I hated this cat. I absolutely hated this cat. As Eleanor talked, I felt a hole open up inside me. I wanted Eleanor to say all those things about me. But I *wasn't* brave. And I *wasn't* adventurous. And as for keeping secrets, my parents never allowed me to have any. My mom says that secrets are bad for the soul. They eat away at the soul until it's just an old full-of-holes blanket that won't keep you warm at night. So there was no way I could compete with this stupid cat.

"You shouldn't touch that cat if it's contagious," I said. "How would you like to have green gunk pouring out of *your* eyes? They probably wouldn't even let you in the PX with that."

"I wash my hands," said Eleanor. She put the cat on her bed in a patch of sunlight and then arranged pillows all around her. What a fuss! And what did the cat do? She just lay there as if this was exactly the kind of treatment she deserved. That's what I mean about cats. Like they own the world!

We tiptoed out of the room. Eleanor washed her hands, and then we went into the living room. I sat on the couch, but Eleanor started her stretching exercises.

"We don't have time for that," I crabbed. "We need to leave for school in a few minutes."

"What's your big rush?" said Eleanor.

"Oh, who cares!"

"No, really. I want to know. What's up?" Eleanor

stopped her stretching exercises and turned her full attention to me. It made me feel a little better.

"I had this talk with my parents last night," I said. "Eleanor! We have got to figure out what the gadget is. It's more important than anything else. It's even more important than uncovering spies." Spying on people we suspected of being spies was our main activity after school. We had already built a hideout for spying by the ice house, and we planned to build more.

"Nothing's more important than uncovering spies," said Eleanor. "Spies are everywhere during wartime. It's our duty to find them and turn them in."

"Well, okay. But after looking for spies, we should try to uncover the mystery of the gadget."

"Oh, I already know all about that," she said. "It's a big bore!" She returned to her exercises. She was practicing backbends. She could stand on her hands and flip over so that her body made a perfect arch. But she couldn't get back up again. I helped push her to her feet.

"How do you know what the gadget is?"

"I overheard the clerk at the PX talking."

"What? What did she say?" I felt like shaking Eleanor to make the answer come out faster.

"It's a super-powered submarine," Eleanor said with a yawn. "We're going to win the war once they make this submarine and attack all the German U-boats."

"A submarine? In the middle of the desert? We're at least three hundred miles from the nearest ocean."

"That's why we've been hearing all those explosions,"

explained Eleanor. "They're blasting a tunnel. All the way from here to the ocean. I heard the clerk at the PX say that."

I looked at Eleanor. A submarine? In the desert? A tunnel? All the way to the ocean?

"That doesn't make a whole lot of sense," I said. "Do you really think that's what it is?"

"Who knows? Who cares?" she said.

"You don't seem very interested in the whole thing," I said. "I mean, if it *is* a submarine, wouldn't you want to find out more about it? See it for yourself?"

Eleanor stopped practicing backbends and sat on the floor, working on her splits.

"Not really," she said, putting her nose to her knee. "I mean, it has nothing to do with us, really. Once they finish it, the war will be over and we can all go home. But until then, you know, who really cares? They could be working on a super-powered submarine or a lawnmower, and it would all be the same to me."

Eleanor was my best friend. But we were as different as salt and pepper. What counted with her counted deeply— friends, family, even her stupid cat. But all the rest didn't amount to a hill of beans.

Most of the other kids on the Hill were like Eleanor. They never talked about the gadget. And when the subject came up, they weren't very interested.

But I couldn't stand not knowing. It was a secret. And secrets eat away at the soul. One way or another, I had to find out. I kept my mouth shut, but I vowed to find out.

9

High Ground

We'd been on the Hill just two months when my mom decided it was time for us to go hiking in the mountains. The whole family. We would get up just after daybreak, drive as far as the road would take us, and then hike up, up, up until we couldn't go any farther. "Until the sun rests like a shawl on our shoulders and the whole world lies at our feet," said my mom. That's when we would eat: baloney sandwiches and hot coffee, sliced apples with cheese, and chocolate cake thick with vanilla frosting. My mom had saved her sugar ration coupons for a month to make that frosting.

The hiking idea was not an original. A lot of the families on the Hill hiked in the mountains almost every Sunday, as long as the weather was good. Especially the Germans and the Italians. They couldn't get enough of hiking.

In fact, it was the Perrottas who had invited us along. Mr. Perrotta didn't work in Dad's division in the Tech Area. He was a stinker, not a fizzler. But he and Dad were great friends anyway.

The Perrottas had come to the United States a few years back, just before things got really bad in Europe. Mrs. Perrotta was Jewish, so they knew they had to get out before it was too late. "We saw the alphabet on the wall," Mr. Perrotta told me once, in his gooey Italian accent. "Dark days, 'Azel." He shook his head sadly. "I pray to God your America never knows such a time of darkness. I pray to God to save my beautiful Italia."

Mr. Perrotta's daughter, Gemma, was in the sixth grade with me and Eleanor. We played Parcheesi with Gemma and climbed trees and looked through movie magazines and even drank Cokes at the PX. But we never showed her our secret hideouts. "*National security*," said Eleanor, arching her eyebrows so high they almost disappeared into her hair. You see, the Italians were the enemy because of Mussolini. So even though there were good Italians, like the Perrottas, there were also bad Italians, like the Fascists. And you just couldn't be too careful when it came to secret hideouts.

On that particular Sunday, my whole family got up with the birds. My mom made the sandwiches and coffee. My dad gathered up extra sweaters and rain gear, just in case. There was a last-minute flurry when my mom couldn't find her security pass. It wasn't in the top drawer of her dresser where she always kept it.

"How can it be gone?" she asked, throwing socks and underpants and slips onto her bed, making a white mountain of cotton and silk. "I never use it!"

It was true. Even though we could leave the Hill for a day whenever we wanted, we never did. It was just too miserable. The only place to go was Santa Fe, and once we got there, we had to follow all the Army's rules. We weren't allowed to talk to anyone. I mean, *anyone*. Not the soda jerk at Woolworth's. Not the sales clerk at the Rexall. Not even the old Indian woman who sold flowers in the town square. If we happened to run into someone we knew, we had to make an excuse and get away as quick as we could. And if anyone asked us where we were from, we had to lie.

To top it all off, we were followed by the G2 the whole time we were off the Hill. Guys in dark suits who watched us to make sure we didn't say the wrong thing to the wrong person. Get my drift? They kept files on all of us. Even the kids.

After our first trip off the Hill, Mom decided it was easier just to stay *on* the Hill. She couldn't stand being followed, and she refused to lie. So *where* was her pass?

We had been searching for more than fifteen minutes when I finally found it stuck in a book on her night table. She had used it as a bookmark by mistake!

Just in time, because that's when we heard the wheezy honk of Mr. Perrotta's old Packard. We climbed inside and rumbled off to the West Gate. There, we met up with two other carloads of people who were going on the hike. The Talbots were there, in their green-and-white DeSoto, and the Beckers in their ancient Model T Ford. As soon as we pulled up, Eleanor hopped out of her car and straight into ours. The three of us—Eleanor, Gemma, and I—sat on the floor in the back seat, our knees pressed up against our chins, trying to stay out of the way of the grownups' feet.

All in all, six families were going on the picnic, along-with Timoshenko, the Hill dog, who somehow always managed to weasel his way into any car that had food in it. I was glad he wasn't in our car. I like dogs, but Timoshenko was a bit smelly in close quarters, if you know what I mean.

Once we were all arranged, we drove up to the West Gate. The guard checked our passes and counted heads. He didn't like it that Eleanor was in our car. He wanted all members of the same family to be in the same car. But Mr. Perrotta and Mr. Talbot refused to give in. They *liked* making life more difficult for the MPs. All the grownups on the Hill did. It was their little game. Sort of like us digging holes under the fence.

The guard finally gave up. After all, there was no army regulation saying that we had to be grouped by family. But we had put him in a sore mood. He made the driver of each car write on the sign-out sheet exactly where we were going and how long we'd be gone and what was the nature of our business. Mr. Perrotta wrote, "To have some fun," but the guard didn't like that. He crossed it out and wrote "Recreation." I swear, those guards at the gate never smiled at anything.

Once we were through, we drove for almost an hour, following a sort-of road up the side of a mountain. When the cars started to spin their wheels, we left them on a flat part and headed up on foot.

There were twelve grownups and almost as many kids. The climbing was hard, at least it was for me. At first I thought I was the only one who was struggling, but then

I saw that my Dad was breathing hard and sweating buckets. Of course, he was carrying the pack on his back that had our lunch. Eleanor, as usual, was grace in motion. She leaped over rocks and sprang across ditches. Sometimes the hardest thing about being Eleanor's friend was feeling like a dandelion growing alongside a rose.

We followed a beaten-down trail for awhile. But when that ended, we continued anyway, scrambling over rocks, crossing dried-up arroyos, grabbing at scrubby shrubs and each other as we struggled to the top.

Most of the time, no one talked. I could hear breathing and footsteps, a rock falling, a twig snapping. Then suddenly, someone would catch sight of a hawk or a jackrabbit, and we'd all whisper, "Look at that!" and "See, see! Over there." Then more climbing and silence.

Mr. Perrotta led the group. He carried a long walking stick cut from an aspen tree. He used it to pull himself up the mountain and to point out rock formations in the distance.

My legs started to go wobbly after about an hour. What if I can't make it? I worried. Would they leave me behind? I was starting to stray toward the back of the pack. Gemma and Eleanor were thirty feet in front of me. They looked like they could walk for hours.

Just when I was beginning to give up, I heard Mr. Perrotta call out, "Just over this rise. Onward! Onward!" He stopped and encouraged us all up the last steep climb. "Bravo, 'Azel! Bravo," he said. "You look like a goat!"

I staggered over the top and flopped on my back. I closed my eyes for a minute—I just wanted my legs to feel normal again. All the others were shouting, "Breath-taking!" and "Magnificent!" Someone started to sing "O Beautiful for Spacious Skies."

I wobbled over to the edge where everyone else was crowded.

We stood on the west side of the mountain. Below us, the canyon dropped a couple thousand feet. One whole side was covered with groves of trees—golden aspens, rugged piñons. It had been a rainy spring, and now that the first warm days of June were here, the whole canyon was exploding with flowers. Purple and yellow asters covered the mountainside. Juniper and sagebrush tangled with each other. I'd never been able to see so far at once.

My legs were still like rubber bands. I sat down—hard. Mom walked over and sat next to me. Her eyes were wide. Her smile was wider.

"It's just like home," she said.

"Montclair?" I had never seen anything that looked *less* like Montclair in my whole life.

"No, home," she said. "Nebraska. Where Daddy and I grew up."

I had been to Nebraska. It was nothing but flat, flat fields of corn. Corn, corn, and more corn. This was not Nebraska.

"You're loony," I said and squeezed her arm. It was nice to see her so happy.

"No, I'm not. It's the same thing. It's the big open. A world without limits. No edges. Just forever. Didn't you feel that in Nebraska?"

"I guess. If you put it that way."

"There's so much sky. You don't have to search for it, poking between trees or buildings. It's everywhere."

She was right. It *was* everywhere. And it was brighter than the sky back home in Montclair. And bluer and just, more—everything. Think of any word you would use to describe the sky and then multiply it by ten, and that's what the sky looked like that day.

My mom turned slowly around in a circle, looking as far as she could see in every direction.

"You know where my favorite place on earth is?" she asked.

"Where?" I closed my eyes to block out the brightness.

"The horizon," she said.

"That's not really a place," I argued. "The horizon changes, depending on where you stand."

"That's one of the things I like about it," said my mom. "The other thing I like about it is that it's where two worlds come together. The world of rocks and trees and animals and dirt and the world of air and light and clouds and stars. Opposites collide. It's where the ground meets the sky."

"But you can never get there," I said, dissatisfied. "How can you have a favorite place that you can never get to?"

"That's another thing I like about it. It makes it perfect."

My mom spread her arms out to the side and ran a few yards. Did she really think she might take off?

"If I were going to build a church," she said. "I would do it here. In a high place. In *this* high place."

She picked up a stick and stuck it into the ground. It wobbled, then leaned, way over to the left. "I hereby declare this spot as the First Church of the Humanitarian Spiritualists. Let's eat!"

The others had already spread out their blankets and opened up their packs. We soon formed a big noisy group all smushed on too few blankets. Moms and dads and kids, all talking, all reaching for the mustard or another brownie. There was a big fight for the last chocolate chip cookie between my dad and Mr. Perrotta. But guess who got it? Timoshenko, of course. He just jumped up like he always did and snatched it right out of Mr. Perrotta's hand.

But once we were all filled up, things changed. It was sort of like watching a chemical precipitation in a test tube. From the jumble of the group, each element began to separate. First, it was the kids. The younger ones went off to dig in the dirt beside a large rock. The older boys began a game of catch with a baseball they'd brought. Eleanor and Gemma and I began to scour the ground. We were hoping to find bones or maybe an old arrowhead.

And then the dads began to group and separate. They wandered off a little from the moms. They bent their heads together. They drew diagrams in the air. They spoke quietly and wandered still farther away from the group. They were talking about it. The gadget. It had followed them all the way up the mountain.

And so the moms were left, under the low tree, gathering up the leftovers and talking among themselves.

I looked at my mom. She was watching my dad. She looked sad, but peaceful. Then she lay on her back and stared at the great open sky above her. She was in church.

10

The Dinner Guest

Why my mom decided to roast a chicken on one of the hottest days in July—in an electric roasting oven, no less!—was beyond me. I guess she really wanted to make Mr. V feel at home. And there's nothing like roast chicken for that.

Mr. V was like Timoshenko. He belonged to no one, so he belonged to everyone. His real name was Joseph Ver-something-or-other, a long Polish name with a lot of k's in it. The kids all called him Mr. V, and so did a lot of the grownups. I bet the army liked that! Another code name!

Mr. V didn't have any family on the Hill. His wife and two daughters were still in Poland. You see, Mr. V was in England giving a lecture when the Nazis took over Poland way back in '39. He tried to get home, but the Nazis wouldn't let him back into the country. Meanwhile, his wife and two daughters weren't allowed out. So there they were. His wife and kids were stuck inside and he was stuck outside, and they had no way to get in touch with each other. That happened to a lot of families in Europe during the war. They got separated, and then they had to wait until the war ended to find each other again.

Mr. V had troubles all right. I could see that he did. I

guess that's why he was invited to someone's house for dinner pretty much every night of the week. Folks on the Hill were pretty good about that, taking care of each other. Especially a lonely fizzler like Mr. V, so far from home, missing his family and all.

Well, come July, it was *our* turn to have Mr. V over for dinner. Like I said, it was hot, and my crazy mom had been cooking since noon, so the kitchen was just about three hundred degrees Fahrenheit.

"I'm positively wilted," said my mom, peeling off her apron and shaking the wrinkles out of the skirt of her cotton dress. "But the cooking is done. Let's sit on the porch and have a lemonade. I'm sure your dad and Mr. V will be here soon."

We waited and waited and waited. The sun went down, which felt good. But my mom got edgy, which felt bad.

It was almost eight o'clock before we heard footsteps and voices. I ran to the edge of the porch and leaned over. It was Dad and Mr. V all right. Talking, arguing. Mr. V was using both arms to draw something in the air, a curve or an angle, I couldn't tell. My dad was shaking his head. No, no, he didn't agree with Mr. V.

When Dad saw me, he looked surprised. And for a second I saw in his eyes—just for a second—a look as if he didn't know who I was. The truth was, I'd hardly seen him for weeks—no, months. He was always at work in the Tech Area. But the next second he was on the porch and kissing the top of my head.

"I'm sorry we're late, Anna," said my dad. "We just got completely entangled with a new problem."

"Another problem?" asked my mom, rising to greet them. She shook her skirt again, and I could tell she was trying to shake out more than wrinkles. Her irritation, I guess. Mom didn't like to hold onto her bad feelings. She tried to let go of them as soon as she could. "It seems like the Tech Area spawns more problems than solutions, these days."

"Sadly, that is true," replied Mr. V. He looked very old to me, that night. His hair was all gray and he had enormous pouches under his eyes, like a sad old bloodhound. I knew that he was about the same age as my dad, but his troubles made him look older.

"Hello, Miss Hazel," he said, leaning over to pat my shoulder. "That's a lovely scarf you're wearing."

"I'm not wearing a scarf," I said.

"But of course you are. Look in the mirror."

I ran into the house to look in the mirror that hung over the fireplace. In the reflection, I saw a beautiful light blue chiffon scarf wound around one of my braids. It was tied in a bow.

"How did you do that?" I shrieked, delighted. Mr. V was known for his slight-of-hand tricks. I'd seen him pull rocks out of kids' ears and even a bunch of asters from under Oppie's porkpie hat.

The grownups all walked into the living room. I untied the scarf and handed it back to him.

"No, no. For you," he said.

My mom brought out several trays of puffy things and stuffed things, while Dad poured the drinks—scotch for the grownups and root beer for me.

"Won't you sit down?" my mom asked Mr. V. He was standing in the middle of the room, plucking absent-mindedly at the lapel of his jacket. He seemed very uncomfortable, all of a sudden.

"Ah, it is unforgivably rude of me, my dear Anna," he began. "But if I could, for just one moment, listen to the radio."

"Of course! Please! Make yourself at home."

With surprising speed, for such an old guy, he crossed the room to our big RCA and turned the knob. A high whistling noise filled the room along with loud pops and crackles. A voice selling aftershave lotion shouted at us, then disappeared. Another voice—Kate Smith singing "God Bless America"—exploded, then was gone. Mr. V leaned closer to the radio as he slowly turned the knob.

There was another splash of music, and then suddenly but clearly we heard the warm honey tones of the BBC. I didn't even catch what the British newscaster was saying, because Mr. V snapped off the radio before he had said more than a few sentences. He looked entirely relieved.

"I just wanted to make sure it was still there," he said.

"What?" I asked, bewildered.

"London," he said, as he walked over to my dad to accept the offered drink.

The talk during dinner was all of the ongoing water shortage on the Hill and whether or not the addition to the Central School would be finished in time for September classes and the current scandal involving a group of WACs who had been a bit too friendly with the enlisted men—and did money change hands? And what should be done about it? The usual grownup stuff. I listened some and daydreamed some.

When the dishes were cleared, but the coffee not quite ready, there was a sudden uproar in the street. We heard the clanging of the fire bell and the roar of a truck as it sped past our house. There was a fire! We all rushed out to the front porch. People from all the houses spilled out into the street. Fires were pretty common on the Hill. What else could you expect with all those wooden houses and raging coal furnaces? Still, a fire was a big deal, especially for us kids.

I turned to ask my dad if I could chase after the crowd that was chasing after the fire truck. His face looked like it was cut from white marble. Then we heard the fire whistle blow, a signal telling us what part of town the fire was in. Three blasts meant the Tech Area was on fire.

One whistle. Two. Three. As soon as the fourth whistle blew, my dad's face relaxed. He took his handkerchief out of his pocket and mopped his forehead.

"Not tonight, eh, Paul?" said Mr. V. "Not tonight."

"No, thank God."

"Can I go to the fire?" I asked.

But before my dad could answer, my mom said no. "It isn't right, Hazel," she said, "to make a spectacle out of someone's tragedy. We'll go by in the morning and see how we can help the poor family." I kicked the porch railing. Everyone else got to go.

After the grownups had coffee, I went to my room to read. I heard my mom doing the dishes and the quiet hush-hush voices of my dad and Mr. V. And then I heard the screen door bang shut. All of a sudden, I realized that I had forgotten to thank Mr. V for the blue chiffon scarf.

I ran into the living room. My mom was still in the kitchen, humming quietly while she dunked the dishes in the sink. My dad and Mr. V were sitting on the porch. I could see the soft glow on, glow off of their pipes as they sat smoking in the dark. I didn't mean to eavesdrop. I really didn't. But something about their voices made me stop, and then crouch down silently in the shadows.

"Will you sign it, then?" asked my dad.

"No, I don't think so," said Mr. V. "I'm ashamed to say that I'm not really the petition-signing type."

"Neither am I. But this is different. I'm finding it hard to sleep at night, knowing what lies ahead."

"Who knows what lies ahead, Professor?" I imagined Mr. V smiling in the dark, but I couldn't see him. "Perhaps all our efforts will be fruitless. Perhaps we will never, as the kids say, 'get it to go.'"

"Do you think we can build it?" asked my dad.

There was a long silence. So long, I wondered if Mr. V had heard the question.

"Yes," he said, finally. "Yes."

"Then you must sign the petition! It's our only hope! My God, imagine what will happen if the army actually gets its hands on this thing."

"The army already has its hands on this thing, Paul. Are you forgetting who brought us here? Who pays our meager salaries? Who supplies us with water and groceries and cyclotrons and Van de Graaf generators, not to mention nickel beer at the PX?"

Their voices were nothing more than whispers. But even I could tell they were talking about something they shouldn't. I strained to listen in the pitch black.

"But we're still in control now. *We* are. The scientists. Not the army."

"Ah. The head instead of the hands, you mean."

"Yes. I suppose, although it sounds simplistic. We are the head. We are the ones, the only ones, who can build this thing. And we are the only ones who really understand what it means."

"But my dear Paul. We are *not* the only ones. In Germany there is a head, and many hands, too. And they are working just as furiously as we are. What if Hitler builds it first? What then of your petition?"

"Well, of course, then all bets are off."

Mr. V laughed. "What a charming way of putting it. Yes! All bets are off!" He puffed on his pipe for a minute. "Ach! It is too horrible to think of a monster like Hitler having such a monstrous device in his monstrous hands."

They sat in silence for so long, I thought their conversation must be over. I was starting to creep back to my bed when I heard my dad's voice.

"My mother always told me that everyone is born with

a gift. Everyone. My little sister, for example, could play the piano brilliantly. That was her gift, and she made the most beautiful music. And me? I had the gift of my intelligence. And I always knew that someday I would make something beautiful with that. I never imagined this."

"None of us ever imagined that the world would come to this," said Mr. V quietly. "But here we are. And what do we do? All my life, I have been a pacifist. I have not struck another human being since I was six years old. But I tell you, if I had Hitler in front of me today, I would wrap my hands around his neck and squeeze until I had wrung the last drop of life from his miserable body. I want my wife and daughters back. And I will do anything—I am speaking the truth, *anything*—to get them back to me."

"But how do you sleep at night?" asked my dad. His voice was thin like the air.

"I find, my good friend, that I am becoming psychically numb. One more atrocity? What is that? Add it to the pile. This hideous war is making me care less and less about the ideals I once held closest to my heart. Besides, who needs to sleep? I came here to work."

When I heard their chairs scrape back, I started crawling on all fours toward my bedroom. That's when I bumped into my mom's legs. I'm not sure how long she had been standing there in the dark. But I suddenly realized that I hadn't heard the sound of water in the sink for a while.

"Straight to bed," she whispered.

I scurried ahead, and she followed. As she smoothed the sheet over me, she said, "It isn't right to listen to other people's conversations when they don't know you're there."

"I know," I said. "I didn't mean to. It was all a mix-up."

"Even in the middle of a mix-up, you should try to do the right thing." She walked over to my window and lowered it halfway. In July, the days were blistering, but the nights could be cold. Then she sat again on the edge of my bed. "Did you learn anything useful?" she asked.

"I'm not sure," I said. "I'll have to think about it."

"Good. You think about it. Good night."

On hot summer days, my mom's kiss feels cool. In the middle of winter, her kisses are warm. How does she do that?

11

Headlines

One night, I dreamed I looked in the window of Gamma Building, and there was a giant metal robot that looked just like Hitler. I was so scared, I couldn't move. I couldn't even yell. My dad was there, and he was proud. "You've got to fight fire with fire!" he said in my dream. His face was stretched in some weird way. He didn't look like himself. It was him, but it wasn't. It was just the most awful thing. I woke up choking for air.

Was *that* what the gadget was? A robot? What could be so terrible that it would scare my dad?

I decided to stake out the Tech Area guardhouse on the chance that I might overhear an important conversation. After all, that's where the dads came and went. I might catch a few words that could set me on the right track.

I told Eleanor about my plan. She wasn't very enthusiastic—Eleanor never loved stakeout work—but she was a friend to the end, so she came along. After three days, we hadn't uncovered even one clue, and the MPs were getting really mad at us. Even our favorite MP, Sergeant McElway, was fed up. He was from Georgia and very polite, which most of the MPs were not. He called me Miss Hazel and tipped his helmet, like I was a real lady. But on the third day of our stakeout, he told us to *am-scray or else*.

"What now?" asked Eleanor.

I could see she was hoping I was ready to give up. She'd never cared about the gadget to begin with. Eleanor didn't have dreams about Hitler robots. She dreamed about Jimmy Stewart and Lana Turner. Eleanor dreamed in Technicolor.

"I guess we'll just lie low for a while," I said.

Eleanor looked relieved. I heard her whisper, "TGTBT."

The next day was Sunday. Eleanor and her parents were gone for the whole day. They were having lunch in Santa Fe and going to a matinee. I knew I shouldn't have hoped for it, but I had sort of been wondering if they would invite me along. Stupid. It was a family thing.

My dad wasn't home, even though it was his day off. Something was going on in the Tech Area. Something that was driving him crazy. Lately, he'd been spending evenings lying on the living room couch, staring at the ceiling. Counting nails, he said. It was driving my mom nuts.

I kicked around the apartment all morning, leaving a mess wherever I went and grumbling a lot.

"Would you cut it out!" my mom exploded. "Find something to do or go outside." She was rolling piecrusts like a madwoman. There was a lecture meeting that night, and Mom had volunteered to bring the eats. The Lecture Committee was her favorite club on the Hill, so she was really going all out. She even had Black Beauty fired up.

"It's a million degrees outside," I complained. "If I go out, I'll fry like a lizard."

"Well, it's a million and ten degrees in here, and if you spend one more minute moping I'm going to bean you with this rolling pin. Find something to do!"

"There's nothing," I whined, hating myself for whining but not able to stop.

"Read a book! Write a letter! Dust the living room! Sweep the floor! Anything!"

"Ma-a-a."

"Unpack the Mystery Boxes. There. Do that."

"Ha, ha," I said.

"I mean it. Pick one and unpack it. You never know what you might find."

The Mystery Boxes were a family joke. There were four of them in a corner of the kitchen. Four cardboard boxes that my mother had packed up in Montclair. But we'd never unpacked them. At first, we'd all been too busy. Then, we'd just lost interest. "If you can live without something for four months and never miss it," my mom said, "it must not be anything you really need." So there they sat, the Mystery Boxes, month after month.

"Pick one," said my mom.

I chose the one that bulged. Inside were dozens of china teacups and saucers, my granny's old set. Each hand-painted piece was wrapped in a page of newspaper, so that by the time I'd finished unpacking the set, I had a stack of crumpled pages and hands as black as night.

"What was I thinking?" said my mom, shaking her

head. "That I'd be throwing tea parties here?" The dainty cups and saucers looked ridiculous on our army-issue wool rug.

I reached down to pick up the crumpled newspapers when I noticed a date at the top of a page.

"Mom, this is the *New York Times,* exactly one year ago today. Look. August 6, 1943."

"Now that's eerie, that you opened that box today, of all days," said my mom, throwing more wood into Black Beauty's hold. "Read some. Let's hear what the world was up to a year ago today."

I spread all the newspaper pages out on the floor. It was like a puzzle. In less than five minutes, I had the whole first section of the paper together.

"Listen to this," I said, sitting down at the kitchen table where my mom was rolling out another crust. The kitchen was hotter than Hades, but it sure smelled good. There were two apple pies cooling on the windowsill and two more in the oven. The room smelled like spices and sugar and good times before the war.

I read aloud a short article at the top of the front page. It was about the fighting at Guadalcanal. That was at the beginning of the war. A lot of Americans had died there. But the article didn't mention that. It said that 40,500 Japanese were killed during the campaign.

"The Army officer added that while the Japanese were good as jungle fighters they were far from being supermen, and that 'man for man we'll beat the Jap anywhere,' " I read.

My mother shook her head and made a *tsk*ing sound with her tongue against her teeth. She didn't like the word *Jap*.

"Go on," she said.

I plunged into the main headline of the day. It was a long article about the Allied fighting on three fronts: The British had seized Catania, a city somewhere in Sicily. The Russians had won back Belgorod, which I figured from the article was somewhere in the Soviet Union. And the Americans were in Munda, a region somewhere in the southwest Pacific.

"The German strongholds of Orel and Belgorod fell yesterday to powerful Russian armies scoring their greatest summer triumph of the war, and Premier Joseph Stalin spurred his troops on westward today with the cry 'Death to the German invaders!' " I read.

The article was full of good news for the Allies. In fact, there was so much good news, you would have thought the war was going to end any day. But this was news from a year ago. And the war was still raging on all fronts.

"Okay. Here's one about Germany," I said. " 'Hamburg Center Stricken.' Should I read it?"

My mom sucked in her breath. "Do you remember the bombings in Hamburg?"

"Oh, sure," I said. It had been a big campaign last summer. For weeks and weeks, the Americans had dropped bombs on the city all day and then the Brits had taken over at night. It was called 'round-the-clock bombing. "We destroyed the shipyards, didn't we?"

I said. I didn't remember much more than that.

"Hamburg was a terrible tragedy," said my mom. "Do you remember reading about the firestorms there?"

"You mean fires from the bombs?"

"It was more than that," said my mom. "Could you get five eggs from the icebox? I'm making a meringue."

"In this heat?" I asked. "I wouldn't count on it."

The blast of cold air from the icebox hit my sweaty body like a freight train. A shiver ran all the way down me. I handed her the eggs. They felt wonderfully cool and smooth, like something from an alien planet.

Crack. My mom expertly separated the yolk from the white. The egg white slithered out of the shell like something alive. Crack. Crack.

"What happened in Hamburg was something the world had never seen before," she said. "All the bombing, day after day, night after night, caused little fires to start all over the city. The wind made the fires grow bigger and bigger. And when the hot air from the fires rose, almost in a column, it sucked in air from outside. That made the fires burn even hotter. And this just kept going and going, so that more and more air was pulled in. Finally the winds reached hurricane force, turning the whole city into a raging firestorm. Can you imagine that, Hazel? Being in a hurricane of fire? People in Hamburg who weren't even near the fire were melted. Not burned by the fire. Their bodies melted from the heat."

"Sort of like this kitchen," I said. I didn't mean to sass, but the kitchen was really hot, and the bombing in Hamburg—it had happened a year ago.

My mom wiped her forehead with a kitchen towel and then nodded toward the newspaper as a signal for me to go on reading. She threw a fistful of flour onto the kitchen table. It scattered in a puff, like an explosion. Then she took another ball of dough from the icebox and started to roll it out.

"The latest Royal Air Force raid on Hamburg was directed principally against the center of the city," I read, "completely wrecking the opera, Rathaus and Gaensemarkt quarter. Evacuation was in full swing, with crowded trains leaving all day long from Dammtor station. Money was no longer needed in Hamburg for trains or buses."

I turned the newspaper over to read the rest of the article. My hands left damp marks on the page.

"Heartrending scenes were reported by Danish evacuees. Hordes of children orphaned by the raids or out of touch with their parents were wandering aimlessly about the streets." I stopped.

"Keep reading," said my mom. She had finished arranging the crusts in the two pie plates and was filling them with dried beans. Once the beans covered the bottoms of the empty crusts, she popped them both in the oven and started to wipe down the table.

The newspaper wilted in my hands, but I straightened it out. "At the Danish border, a twelve-year-old boy, traveling alone and carrying two sacks, was asked by the customs officers to open the sacks. One revealed the corpse of his two-year-old brother, killed in the raid. In the other sack were the boy's rabbits."

I shifted in my chair. I could feel my blouse sticking to my back. Two little rivers of sweat ran down the sides of my face, past my ears.

My mother stopped her cleaning. She was looking at me, but I kept staring at the newspaper.

"What are you thinking?" she asked.

I didn't know what to say. That boy was just about my age. But then again, he was German. He was the enemy.

"I guess it's okay," I said. "Because it's the Germans, right? I guess we want all the Germans to die."

"We want the war to end, Hazel," said my mother. "We don't want little babies burned to death. Not even German babies. Do you understand that?"

"But *they* killed babies and old people. Lots of people died in London during the Blitz. Just regular people."

"Does that make it right?" she asked. "Just because the Germans killed innocent people, it isn't right for us to do the same. Even in the name of war. I know that's not a popular point of view right now. But we can't spend our lives trying to outdo each other with cruelty."

My mom went to the sink and rinsed out the dirty rag in a trickle of water. The General was constantly sending us bulletins about water conservation. It was a top priority on the Hill.

My mom turned from the sink to look at me. "War ... ," she said. "War doesn't make sense. But somewhere, someone has to stand up for what is right. And killing children—even enemy children—isn't right. It's a lifelong struggle, but we have to reach a higher plane, Hazel. A better place. A better place where we respect all life."

I looked at my mom. She had tears in her eyes. She looked like she thought I might start crying. But me, I don't cry. I looked at my dirty hands, then I asked to be excused.

I went into the bathroom and washed my hands, using twice as much water as I needed. I had to scrub to get the newsprint off, and still my nails were rimmed with black.

I went into my room and lay on my bed. Where was that boy now? A year ago today he'd been wandering the countryside of Denmark. No parents. No brother. No home. Where was he now?

After dinner, I heard the Talbot's car pull up and Eleanor and her parents climb the stairs to their apartment. I followed a few minutes later to hear about their day. Then Eleanor and I built a house of cards seven stories high, and we whooped and hollered so loudly that Mrs. Talbot came running into the bedroom to see if we were okay.

It's hard to hold on to someone else's pain. It's like those egg whites in the bowl. It just slithers away.

12

Madame Curie, I Presume

Our entire sixth-grade class was promoted to the seventh grade—all ten of us. Since the high school and the grade school were all in the same building, it didn't seem to make much difference. We just moved from one classroom down the hall to another.

But we no longer had Miss Burrows as our teacher. Now we had different teachers for each subject. Mrs. Smith taught history. Mrs. Wilson taught English. Mrs. Inglis taught math. We didn't have a science teacher. The idea was that twice a week one of our famous scientist dads would give a lecture. But they kept canceling. The pace in the Tech Area had picked up. There was always a crisis over there, and the dads couldn't just up and leave to give a lecture to a bunch of high-school kids. So week after week, our science class was just a filmstrip. Or some sort of experiment cooked up by the school principal, Mrs. Crouch. I don't think I learned a thing in science that whole year.

So we were walking home one day—Eleanor, Gemma, and I—that first week of seventh grade. Eleanor had *finally* gotten her mom to give her permission to wear polish on her toenails—she'd been working on her mom for weeks—

and Gemma and I were trying to figure out some way to get our moms to let us wear it, too. Eleanor even had a bottle of Maybelline polish stashed in her underwear drawer: *Victory Red*. She said that *Victory Red* was the color Gene Tierney wore in the movie *Laura*. I asked her how she knew that since the movie was in black and white, and she said that she had read it in *Modern Screen*.

Then we got to talking about last year and Miss Burrows and whether she was average-smart or genius-smart. Gemma thought she was genius-smart, like our dads.

"Not on your life," I said. I know genius-smart when I see it, and Miss Burrows wasn't it.

"Well, I hope for her sake that she isn't all that smart," said Eleanor, "because smart women have a *much* harder time finding husbands."

"What d'ya mean?" I asked.

"It's simple," said Eleanor. "When you're talking about marriage, the husband always has to be smarter than the wife. So-o-o, the smarter the woman is, the harder it is for her to find a husband who is *even smarter*. It's just a question of math," she said, flipping her black hair over her shoulder.

"Why can't the woman be smarter than the man?" I asked.

"It just doesn't work," said Eleanor. "The marriage won't last. It just falls apart. Trust me. I know what I'm talking about." She had read an article in *Ladies Home Journal* that said just that. "And besides, look at our moms and dads. The dads are all much smarter."

Deep in my heart, I knew she was wrong, but she had all the evidence on her side.

"But that's not fair!" I shouted. I was really mad now. Mad at Eleanor. Mad at that stupid magazine. Mad at the whole dumb world.

"Relax, Hazel," said Eleanor. "You don't have to worry. I'm talking about girls who are super smart. Like right-off-the-chart smart. They're doomed."

All I'd ever wanted was to be like the other kids. Average. Ordinary. Regular. I should have been happy. But I was mad.

"Oh yeah?" I said. "Well supposing the husband doesn't know that the wife is smarter? Supposing she keeps it a secret for their whole marriage."

Eleanor rolled her eyes like I had just said something really stupid. When it comes to love, Eleanor thinks she's an expert, just because a boy once kissed her. *On the cheek*. Big deal!

"Hazel. Marriage is *forever*. A person can't fake being dumb forever. And once the husband finds out, it's over. *Kaput*."

By now, I was boiling mad. I mean, what kind of a world was this? Why did it have to be this way? How come it was the smart people—the smart *girls*—who got teased and picked on and didn't even get to choose whether or not they wanted a husband?

"Well, first of all, *Miss Know-It-All*"—I said that part really sarcastically—"anyone who believes everything she

reads in the *Ladies Home Journal* is incredibly gullible."
(I knew she'd have to look that word up once she got
home.) "And furthermore, Marie Curie was *much* smarter
than Pierre Curie. So there."

Last Saturday, Eleanor and I had gone to see the
picture *Madame Curie* in Theater No. 2, and we both
loved it. When Marie and Pierre saw that lump of radium
glowing in the laboratory after all those years of work, I
had to grab hold of my chair to keep from standing up
and cheering. And then when Marie found the earrings
that Pierre had bought for her just before he died, Eleanor
cried so hard she got hiccups. It was the greatest picture
we'd ever seen.

"Well, anyone who believes everything she sees in the
movies is even more *gubbible*," shot back Eleanor.

And then I called her a moron, and she called me an
idiot.

By this time, we were in front of our apartments, and
Eleanor stomped up to hers and I stomped in to mine.
I'm pretty sure that Gemma followed Eleanor upstairs
after I had gone inside. Which just goes to show you.

I slammed the door and threw my book bag on the
floor. Then I flopped on the couch, making sure my shoes
hung over the edge. My mom walked into the living
room from the bedroom. She had been writing a letter. I
could tell because she had a pen in her hand and her face
had that thinking-of-faraway-places look that she gets
whenever she writes letters home.

"Don't you have some sort of meeting today?" I asked

in a crabby voice. Sometimes, you just want to be alone. "I thought Friday was Sewing Club day, or something like that."

"It is. But I decided to skip this week."

"Huh!" I had no idea what I meant by that, but I was upset and didn't want to talk.

My mom just stood there for a couple of minutes. I kept kicking the leg of the coffee table.

"Troubles?" she asked.

"Oh, what's the difference?" I said and ran into my bedroom. I slammed the door shut and lay face down on my bed.

A minute later I heard a soft knock on my door. I pretended not to hear.

"Hazel?" said my mom. "Can I come in?"

"I'd just rather you didn't," I said, my throat all hot and tight.

"It might make you feel better if you talk about it," she said.

"No! No. I don't want to talk about it. It's just stupid, and I don't want to even think about it."

"But if you. . ." said my mom.

"Could you *please* just leave me alone?" I tried to say it nicely. I know it didn't sound very nice.

I heard her footsteps on the wooden floor going down the hall until they were swallowed up by the living room rug.

Twice that afternoon, I had my hand on the doorknob. I *wanted* to talk to my mom. More than anything else, I wanted to talk to her, just like I did back home. But what could I say? That I'd been pretending to be dumb at school? That my best friend thought I was dumb enough to catch a husband? My mom would be so disappointed. She couldn't stand phonies.

So I spent the whole afternoon by myself, playing solitaire and building houses of cards. I never got past the third story.

By the next morning, I wasn't even mad anymore. Eleanor was Eleanor. And I was—I wasn't sure who I was anymore. I sat up in my bed and tried to think of what to do.

What do you do when you've had a fight with your best friend and you want to make up? Should I go upstairs and say I'm sorry? Should I pretend like nothing happened? Or should I wait and see if Eleanor was still mad? What if I *did* apologize and she told me I was a jerk and she never wanted to see me again? That would be even worse than fighting.

I looked out my window to check the clothesline. There was a note! I grabbed it. This is what it said:

> Knock. Knock.
> Who's there?
> Apologizing friend.
> Apologizing friend who?
> Apologizing friend Eleanor.

Eleanor was Eleanor, I thought to myself. Thank God.

13

Moving Forward

I heard the hum of the clothesline as it ran over its two nails. It was late, past eleven o'clock. My dad still wasn't home from the Tech Area. Maybe he wouldn't be coming home at all tonight. My mom had already gone to bed. I heard her, at least a half-hour ago, punching pillows before she settled down to sleep.

I cracked open the window. A tongue of shivery cold air reached into the room and licked my arm. As quick as I could, I grabbed the white square of paper pinned to the line.

"Super secret mission. Danger level: XXX. Meet me out back at twenty-three hundred hours. (That's now.) — Agent Z"

I heard the rope fall from Eleanor's window, then the muffled thump-thump as she climbed down the wall. I pulled a dirty pair of jeans and two sweaters out of my clothes hamper. Putting on dirty clothes was quieter than opening my dresser drawers for clean clothes. When I landed next to Eleanor, she grabbed my hand and pulled me away from the house.

This wasn't the first time we'd sneaked out at night. But it was the first time since the weather had turned cold. The night air was like cat's claws in my nose. It hurt to breathe. We crept through the pitch black to Mr. Talbot's car—we'd done this before, too—and climbed inside, closing the doors as quietly as we could. Eleanor had some snickerdoodles and a movie magazine and a flashlight, all in a backpack. She had even brought a couple of bed pillows 'cause the car seats were pretty hard. She divvied up the cookies, and we started looking at the pictures of movie stars.

"Cripes! I got a nut stuck in my tooth," she said. She grabbed the flashlight from my hand and flipped down the sun visor to look in the mirror. Something jangled to the floor. She flashed the light down and picked up something in the darkness.

"Wanna see me drive?" she asked with a wicked grin on her face. She held up the keys that had fallen from the visor.

"You can't drive," I said.

"Oh, yes I can," she said. "Summers on my grandpa's farm since I was eight. Not just cars, either. Tractors."

She put the key in the ignition, pulled out some doohickey lever, pressed her left foot on a pedal, and turned the key. The engine came alive. At first it snarled like an angry lion, but then it settled into a yes-indeedy purr.

I couldn't move, I was so terrified. But Eleanor was a cool cat. She adjusted the rearview mirror, pushed some lever thing, and pressed on a different pedal with her right foot. As smooth as silk, the car rolled away from the house.

"You can't do this!" I said.

"What do you mean?" she said. "I'm doing it!"

"I mean, you can't take your dad's car! It's stealing!"

"Hazel!" And even though it was dark, I could tell she was rolling her eyes at me. "You can't steal from your own dad! That's the law. Trust me. I know what I'm talking about."

"You do *not* know what you're talking about," I squeaked. "And you're gonna get us in the biggest trouble of our lives!"

She was looping the car around Ashley Pond, just as pretty as you please. Every second, I expected the MPs to come down on us. Or at least Eleanor's parents. But no one came. Nothing happened.

"Let's head toward the West Gate," she said. "The road there is straight."

I felt as though all the oxygen had been sucked out of the car. I could hardly see I was so scared. But on the straight road, I calmed down a little. Eleanor was a good driver, slow and careful. Why should I be surprised? Another thing that Eleanor was good at.

About a mile from the West Gate, she turned the car around and then cut the engine.

"Your turn," she said, climbing over me and wedging herself between me and the door.

I looked at her like she had horns growing out of her head.

"Come on. It's easy. *Trust* me."

"I can *not* drive!" I said, slapping at her hands that

were pushing me toward the steering wheel. "I'm too short, and I don't know how, and I'm twelve years old!"

"You can do it," she urged. "Have a little faith. I'll tell you everything you need to know."

My hands were on the wheel. The wheel was huge and smooth and icy cold. My feet just reached the pedals, but I couldn't see over the hood of the car. I was too short.

"Here," said Eleanor, sliding the pillows under my rear. "Now you're as tall as me."

Using the flashlight, Eleanor pointed out the gas pedal, the brake, and the clutch. Then she showed me how to move the stick shift from neutral into first gear.

"That's all you need to know for now," she explained.

I spent the next ten minutes stalling out the car. This isn't so bad, I thought. At least we're not going anywhere.

But on the forty-seventh try, the car leaped forward.

"Easy, easy on the clutch," shouted Eleanor. "Give it some gas! You're doing great."

"I don't know how to steer!" I yelled.

"It doesn't matter," said Eleanor. "There's nothing to hit out here."

She was right. All around us was nothing but flat blackness. Somewhere out there was the fence that surrounded the mesa, but we were at least a mile from that. I kept a light hand on the steering wheel and basically let the car do whatever it wanted. This was my philosophy of driving.

The car decided to veer off the dirt road and onto the mesa. We rolled forward about a hundred yards into the darkness, and then I panicked and slammed on the brakes. The engine cut out.

"You're a natural!" crowed Eleanor. "Try it again."

My palms were sweating and my whole body had the shakes, but I wanted to try again. This time, the engine caught on just the third try.

"You are so much better at this than I was when I first learned," said Eleanor. (I knew she was lying. Eleanor is going to be a great cheerleader when she gets back to a normal high school with a football team.)

For the next half-hour, Eleanor coached me. I drove straight. I drove in circles. I even drove a figure eight. At one point, the speedometer hit fifteen miles per hour.

"Let's take her home," Eleanor finally said, yawning. "We don't want to use up too much gas. It's unpatriotic. And my dad will kill me."

"I'm not driving it into town," I said.

"Sure you are. Just take it slow. You're a *natural*."

We couldn't even find the dirt road until we were almost at the edge of town. Most of the houses were dark. A few lights still burned in the Tech Area. I wondered if my dad had come home or if he was sleeping at the lab. I inched along at five miles per hour. The car hardly made a sound. It was very peaceful. My mind wandered.

All of a sudden, there was water in front of me. Black water rushing up to the car. I slammed on the brakes. The car skidded and then sputtered out. Eleanor woke up with a yelp. We looked out over the hood.

The car was pointing straight at Ashley Pond. One of

the front tires was over the edge of the bank, hanging in thin air. Neither of us said anything for a full minute. We listened for MPs on foot, in jeeps, on horseback. We expected the whole patrol to come down on us any minute.

"I think I should drive the rest of the way," said Eleanor. We changed places, and she backed the car away from the pond. "I'll teach you how to drive in reverse next time."

There will never be a next time, I thought. But there was. And sooner than I thought.

14

In Ruins

After a cold Halloween, the first week of November turned crazy warm. It felt like May all over again. So of course the Italians decided to go hiking. My dad was working, even though it was a Sunday, and my mom said she was too tired for a long hike. But Gemma said I could come anyway. Eleanor was sick in bed with laryngitis. Her mother had wrapped a hot, woolen sock around her throat and wouldn't even let her stick her head outside.

We were most of the way up the trail when Mr. Perrotta stopped Gemma and me. "Look, girls. I promised. Ruins." He pointed across the side of the mountain we were climbing to a spot farther up. We looked and saw rows and rows of caves dug into the side of the mountain. I had brought my dad's binoculars, but still we couldn't see inside the caves from where we stood. Gemma and I wanted to break away from the group right then, but Mrs. Perrotta insisted we eat first. Mothers! I've never gobbled hard-boiled eggs and gingersnaps so fast in my life.

"Can we go now?" I begged Gemma. Her mom waved us away as if we were flies buzzing around her soup.

We started down the slope, but a rough patch of

thorny scrub got in our way. We tried to just charge through the bushes, but they scratched at our legs and tore our pants. We kept going though. We wanted to find bones in those ruins.

All of a sudden, Gemma asked, "So how come your mom quit the Lecture Committee?"

"She didn't," I said. "The Lecture Committee is her favorite club. She'd never quit that."

"My mom is president of the Lecture Committee," said Gemma. "And she says your mom hasn't been to any of the meetings in weeks. *And* she quit the Mesa Club. *And* the Drama Club."

"Well, maybe she's just been busy," I said. What was Gemma getting at, anyway?

"Maybe," said Gemma, shrugging her shoulders. "Hey, don't get mad. I didn't mean anything by it. I was just wondering."

We stopped talking entirely and concentrated on the scratchy branches all around us. But that didn't stop my brain from working. I'd noticed that my mom was around the house a lot. But I'd never bothered to ask her why. I guess if I'd asked, she would have told me. Truth was, I wasn't much around the house myself. When we weren't in school, Eleanor and I were usually outside or in Eleanor's apartment, where there wasn't a watching mother around. Had she really quit the Lecture Committee?

Finally, Gemma and I found a break in the bushes and made our way down toward the caves. There were hundreds of them. Hollowed out chambers, like cells in a honeycomb. The ground here was soft and dry, the color of a peach. With my hand, I could dig into the walls. The earth crumbled through my fingers, soft as silk, light as ashes. Who had lived here? What had they left behind?

Gemma and I began to hunt. The caves were in rows, layered like a cake. To get from one to another, we had to walk on a narrow ledge made out of the same crumbling earth. I held my breath as I walked slowly along the ledge, wishing Eleanor was there to give me courage.

Inside each cave, the air was cool and dry. I learned quickly to walk more carefully so I wouldn't stir up all the dust and dirt that rested on the floor. I found a few broken pieces of pottery. Some smooth black rocks arranged in a circle. No bones.

"Let's climb to the top," suggested Gemma, "and look over." Slowly we made our way to the very top of the cliff. On the other side was a canyon and beyond miles and miles of mesas with deep canyons separating them. Empty mesas, flat and dry, with nothing but trees and dirt and rocks. And then the Hill.

I had never seen the Hill from far away. It looked like an ant hill with its top chopped off. Hundreds of buildings, crowded together on a scrap of flat land. I put the binoculars to my eyes. I could see cars, like insects, crawling over the mesa. And behind the Hill, like a giant mother protecting her little ones, rose the Jemez Mountains and the great Valle Grande. I hadn't realized just how isolated we were on our little Hill in the middle of nowhere.

I shifted my binoculars to the next mesa over. South

Mesa, it was called, and there were a few rough buildings there, too. South Mesa was where most of the explosions happened. All day, every day, except sometimes on Sunday, we heard explosions booming in the canyons. The ground on South Mesa was burned black in spots.

"Why do you think they blow up things, all day long, on South Mesa?" I asked.

"Don't know," said Gemma with a shrug. "My dad says Neddermeyer is a crank." Seth Neddermeyer was the fizzler who was in charge of the explosions. The mothers all cursed him, especially when they were trying to settle little ones down for naps.

"My dad says Neddermeyer is a crank and a genius," I said. "He says those are the people who change the world." I looked again at the charred, burned ground. "It's a miracle no one has been killed on South Mesa." I felt a shiver, even though the sun beat down on us, high as we were. "Let's head back."

Gemma and I hiked to where the grownups were. The dads were readying the backpacks. The moms were counting children. As I walked back to the car, my mind was filled with jumbled bits: the feel of the soft dirt, the cool smoothness of the stones, the burned ground, the sound of my mother crying late one night. Fragments, broken thoughts. All in ruin.

Back in town, the Perrottas offered to drive me home, but I said no, I'd rather walk. I wanted to be alone. But when I got to Ashley Pond, there was a knot of people gathered, and right in the middle was my mom, barefoot and dripping wet. She was kneeling on the ground over something—it looked like a pile of rags—and next to her was a boy. He was soaking wet, too. Out on the water, I noticed one of the canoes. It was overturned and floating in the middle of the pond.

I ran up to them. That's when I saw that the pile of rags was really another boy. It was Severo, from my class. His face was a sickly yellow-white, like old cheese, and his black hair stuck to his cheeks. His eyes were closed, and his mouth was all mushed up. My mom had rolled him over on his side and was hitting him on his back. But he didn't move.

Just then, another boy, also dripping wet, ran up. "He's coming! I found him. He's coming!"

Seconds later, Dr. Coles arrived, carrying his black bag.

Dr. Coles knelt over the boy. "How long was he under the water?" he asked.

"I don't know!" said one of the boys. "Five minutes, I guess. I don't know."

"We were just fooling around," blurted the other boy. "It was a dare! We didn't know he couldn't swim."

"Well now you know," said Dr. Coles. "The boy is dead."

I heard one of the boys whisper, "Oh, we're in Dutch. We're in Dutch, for sure."

My mom was still kneeling next to the body. "Damn canoes," she muttered. "Rotten, full of holes. I should have hauled them to the dump myself." There'd been a petition by the town council to have the canoes removed.

My mom had collected signatures, back in the spring.

I looked at the boy on the ground. It was just like that dream I had with my dad, where his face was stretched and hard to recognize. I looked closer, trying to see the boy I knew. It *was* Severo, but it wasn't.

Suddenly, I thought of the boy from Hamburg. Had he recognized his brother, even after he was dead?

Dr. Coles scooped up the body and said to my mom, "Tell the boy's mother to come to the hospital." He walked away, the two boys following him like dinghies in the wake of an enormous ocean liner.

I walked over to my mom. She was still kneeling on the hard ground.

"I had this dream," she said, "before we came to the Hill. I had this dream. A small child was hurt and I was trying to save him, but I couldn't."

She started to cry, but then shook her head and straightened her shoulders. "Come," she said, standing up. "We need to find where Severo lives. His poor mother. Her heart will break."

15

Making Merry

There were parties on the Hill. Believe me there were parties. Pretty much every weekend, the grownups blew off steam at someone's apartment.

But the Christmas party was different. For one thing, it was hosted by the British Mission—that's what everyone called the scientists and wives that Winston Churchill had sent to the Hill to help make the gadget. So the Christmas party was fancier and more elegant and more, well, more *British* than most Hill parties. It was held on the Saturday night before Christmas in Theater No. 2, and committee moms spent all week decorating the dance hall, baking cakes and cookies, and hoarding gallons of gin and rum for the punch.

Eleanor and I had volunteered to round up the music. That afternoon, we knocked on at least fifty doors, asking to borrow records. We got all the best—Benny Goodman and Glenn Miller and Bing Crosby; Frank Sinatra and Louis Armstrong and Tommy Dorsey. Eleanor put all the Andrews Sisters records on the top of the pile because she was wild for Patty, Maxene, and Laverne. We even got a couple of Kate Smith records, but we shuffled her to the bottom.

We hurried to Theater No. 2 with our wagonload of records to give to the GI who was going to play the music at the party. When we stepped inside, I couldn't believe this was the same place where we watched movies every Wednesday and Saturday night.

Silver and white paper snowflakes hung from the ceiling. And pine branches—yards and yards of them—hung over the doorways, so that the air had that spicy, sharp smell that always reminded me of my first bus ride up the Hill. And in the corner stood an enormous Christmas tree, at least fifteen feet tall, decorated with strands and strands of twinkling lights.

Like a little kid, I ran up to the tree to look at the ornaments. Hundreds of pipettes—thin glass tubes that chemists use for transferring liquids—hung on invisible threads from the tree. They glistened like icicles, catching and reflecting the light. At the very top of the tree, instead of a star or an angel, was a hanging model of a hydrogen atom. The proton was painted silver and covered in glitter. The neutron was gold. The electron and its path were made of a polished silver ring that sparkled as it slowly turned.

"Let's go," said Eleanor. "I want to curl my hair!"

By the time I got home, my mom was stepping out of the shower.

"Oh, for my bathtub in Montclair and a nice long soak!" said my mother. The only bathtubs on the Hill were in the beautiful old cabins on Bathtub Row next to Fuller Lodge. These houses had been part of the private boys' school that was on the Hill before the war. When the war started, the army took over the school, keeping the old buildings and adding new ones. Only bigwigs like Oppie lived on Bathtub Row.

I helped my mom get dressed, just like I did in Montclair. I zipped up her black velvet gown and fastened the garnet necklace that was an heirloom from three generations back on my dad's side.

She sat down at her dressing table and gathered her hair into a glamorous pile on top of her head. I stood next to her, handing her the bobby pins, one at a time. Then she leaned toward the mirror and applied a perfect sweep of dark red lipstick. *Red Flame*, it was called.

Watching her reflection, I had this sudden, crazy feeling. This is hard to explain. Everything felt so familiar, but at the same time completely strange. I almost felt like I could look at my mom as if I didn't *know* her. She looked so beautiful and glamorous and wonderful. Not like my mom. But, of course, she *was* my mom. It was like I had double vision for a second, and saw two people who were the same, but not.

"You're making me nervous, the way you're staring!" said my mom, turning to look at me. I realized all of a sudden that this was the longest we'd been together in months. It was funny, that double vision. It made me feel queer in my stomach.

"You look different," I blurted out.

"Do I?" she asked, turning to look at her reflection in the mirror. She leaned into the mirror and frowned. "You're right. I do look different." She smoothed a single hair away from her face. "To be honest with you, I'm not in much of a party mood."

She stood up. "Now, what about you?" she asked. "You can't wear blue jeans to the Brits' Christmas party."

I had only one party dress, from last winter. It was made of velvet the color of blueberries with yards of crinoline under the skirt. It was small on me, but I squeezed into it. Then my mom brushed and curled my hair and pulled it back with a matching velvet ribbon.

"You look like a dream," said my mom.

Then we sat to wait for my dad. The Tech Area was closing early tonight so all the dads could get ready for the party. But we watched the clock, and he didn't come.

My mom started pacing. A minute later, she said, "Come on."

We put on our coats and walked to the Tech Area. As always, there was a guard at the gate. He stopped my mom as we approached.

"Can I help you, Ma'am?" he asked. The guards, especially the young ones, were always very polite.

"I lost something in the Tech Area."

"I'm sorry. Ma'am. You can't get in without a white badge. Regulations." He pronounced it, "Reg-a-lations."

"Then why don't you go in and find it for me. It's my husband." She was mad. Not at the guard, but he was unlucky enough to be in her way.

The guard didn't even smile. "I'm sorry, Ma'am. I can't leave my post. Regulations."

My mother sized up the guard. I wondered if she was

going to take him on! My heart started to beat faster. Sometimes, you couldn't tell what my mom was going to do.

Just then, a stinker named Kistiakowsky came out of the Tech Area.

"Anna!" he exclaimed. "You're a vision. But why aren't you at the party?" He had a heavy Russian accent, and Eleanor had told me that he had fought in the Czar's White Army.

My mother pointed a grim finger toward the Tech Area.

"I will tear him from his lab table," said Kisty, going back through the gate.

A minute later, my dad came out, pulling on his coat and fighting to get his hat on his head like it was a live cat or something.

"I'm sorry! I'm sorry! I got so involved with this problem we're working on. It's driving us crazy."

All of a sudden, he caught sight of my mother, the look on her face. His hat fell into the snow.

"I'm sorry, Anna."

"One night out of the year," she said, too angry to say more. Then she exploded. "It's like you have a mistress! No, it's worse. You're always stealing time from us to be with her. With it! And you're not even ashamed."

"Anna, please!" said my dad, nodding his head in my direction.

"You think she doesn't know?" said my mom. "Without even knowing it, she knows."

Kisty walked through the gate. "It's snowing!" he

exclaimed. "What a treat for Christmas." He tipped his hat, once to my mother and once to me. "See you ladies at the party."

My mother picked up my father's hat and handed it to him. "Come," she said. "There's a party." We trooped through the falling snow, not one of us making a sound until we were swallowed up by the noise and lights in Theater No. 2.

16

Contraband

Winter settled over the Hill like a bird coming home to roost. One of the mothers kicked off a knitting campaign. Our boys were freezing in foxholes all over Europe, and the only thing we could think of to do was to knit them wool socks.

My problem was I decided to knit a pair of *argyle* socks. Don't even ask me why. I think I wanted my socks to stand out from all the other thousands of pairs shipped overseas. The way air force pilots paint pictures on their planes so they'll stand out in formation. Something like that.

Here's the problem part—every time I try to knit with colors, my yarns get tangled up in an impossible knot. One-color knitting, I'm fine. But the minute I try to knit a pattern, forget it.

By New Year's, I had finished one lumpy sock with a sort of crooked pattern of criss-crossing lines and wobbly diamonds on it. But the other sock was simply refusing to get done. I spent as much time ripping the stitches off the needles as I did putting them on.

One afternoon in early January, I was sitting in the living room trying to untangle *another* knot. The pattern called for five different colors of yarn, and I had all five skeins completely tangled up. I got so mad, I took a pair of scissors and cut out the knot, which was really unpatriotic, because wasting anything during the war—paper, metal, bacon grease, even yarn—was basically treason.

Just then my mom wandered into the living room from the bedroom. She was still wearing her pajamas, and her long hair hung in a loose braid down her back.

"Aren't you going to get dressed?" I asked.

"It's a pajama day," she said, pouring herself another cup of coffee.

"Wasn't yesterday a pajama day?"

"Well, maybe it's a pajama week," she answered sitting on the sofa with her steaming cup. She pulled a newspaper off the top of one of the stacks that cluttered the living room and began to read.

"Mom. That paper's old. I should take them all to the dump today."

"No, don't. I'm still reading them."

"But Mom, they're old. Really old. Some of them are from the summer."

"I still haven't finished reading them," she said, sipping her coffee. "Don't throw them out, yet."

A minute later she added, "Is it cold in here? It feels cold to me."

Actually, the apartment was kind of hot. The coal furnace in the basement had been blasting all morning.

"I'll get Granny's quilt for you," I said. I wrapped her up in the soft familiarity of the Diamond-in-the-Rough pattern. "Are you sick?" I asked.

"No, sweetheart," she said, returning to her paper. "Just tired."

Something made me want to get out of the apartment. Maybe it was the hot, dry air that felt like it was choking me. Or maybe it was my frustration over the sock that lay in a cut-up heap on the floor. Or maybe I was still mad—hurt, to be honest—that both Gemma and Eleanor were off the Hill for the day and neither had asked me along. Or maybe I just didn't like seeing my mother in her pajamas two days in a row.

I buttoned up my coat and pulled on my hat and went out walking. I ended up in our hideout behind the icehouse, which was cold, but at least out of the wind. The hideout wasn't much. It was just a few boards and two empty oil drums that made a lean-to against the back of the icehouse. But we had disguised the opening with a bush (that was my idea) so you really couldn't tell when anyone was inside.

I sat on one of the *Modern Screen* magazines we kept stashed there and tried to think of something to do. Then I heard voices getting closer. I crouched down. From inside the hideout, I could see and hear everything, but I was completely hidden—as long as I didn't move.

It was two boys. Older boys. Seniors at the high school. One boy was short and built like a fireplug. He looked like he could cause some trouble. The other boy was taller and super skinny, with thick wavy black hair and round glasses stuck on his face. He carried a package tucked under his arm like a football. They were so close to the hideout that I could see the postage stamps on the package. I could even make out the familiar words *Opened by the Army Examiner* stamped on the brown paper. He must have just picked up the package at the PX.

"Come on," said the shorter one. "Open it up. No one's around." He reached for the package.

"Get your mitts off," said the taller boy. "I'll open it, if you give me half a chance." He untied the string and opened the box. I was trying to breathe really quietly—they were *that* close to me—and praying I wouldn't sneeze.

First he took out a card. "Happy Birthday. To my darling nephew Simon. Love Aunt Esther."

"I thought you said it was from your friend Jim?" said the shorter one.

"Don't be a noodle," said the taller boy. "Of course it's from Jim, but if he signs it 'Aunt Esther,' it has a better chance of getting past the examiner. Get it?"

"Hey, that's keen," said the shorter boy. "Would you just open the darn thing?" He was hopping up and down like a little kid on Christmas morning.

"You have no sense of the moment," said the taller boy. He shook his head in disgust, but he went back to opening the package.

First he pulled out something wrapped in bright paper with American flags and Uncle Sams all over it. The wrapping was torn, so the army examiner must have already opened the package. The boy quickly ripped off the paper, and there was—

Rats! The short boy blocked my view. I couldn't see

anything! I tried moving quietly inside the hideout to get a better view, but it was no good. What was it? What was in the package?

Then the short boy whistled and stepped back and I could see what the taller boy was holding. It was a Thermos. A red-and-blue Captain Midnight thermos. On the side, I could read the slogan: "Hot Ovaltine, the hearty breakfast!" Both boys stared at it in awe, like they had never seen a Captain Midnight thermos before.

Big deal, I thought to myself. I could order one of those from the back of a comic book.

The taller boy unscrewed the top of the thermos and dumped it upside down. Something wrapped in black velvet slid out.

Now I was curious. *Very curious.* The boy held that package as if it contained the answer to all his prayers.

"I can't believe it made it past the examiner!" squeaked the shorter boy. He was hopping like a grasshopper now. I wondered if he was going to wet his pants.

But the taller boy stood perfectly still, feeling the weight of the velvet-wrapped package, first in one hand and then the other.

What could it be? I wondered. It was definitely contraband because they were worried about the examiner. Was it a bottle of alcohol? Cigarettes? A gun?

I held my breath. The boys stood motionless.

And then Timoshenko came out of nowhere. Like a streak of white light he raced toward the boys, snapped the velvet package into his mouth and was off, hoping for a good game of chase and tackle.

"What the . . . ?" shouted the shorter boy, but the taller boy was already after the dog.

As soon as the boys started after him, Timoshenko really took off. In a flash, he slipped under a hole in the fence and stood on the other side, wagging his tail, waiting for the boys to follow. But the hole was small, hardly big enough for a little kid. There was no way those boys could get through.

"Timmy! Timmy!" coaxed the taller boy. "Come on, boy. Bring it back, boy. Bring it back under the fence." But Timoshenko didn't move.

"Guess what, Timmy? Guess what I have in my pocket?" The boy pulled out a half-eaten sandwich. He held it out for Timoshenko to sniff. Timoshenko dropped the velvet package and trotted toward the fence. Halfway there, he heard the sound of horses' hooves. Like a shot he was off, heading for the woods.

But the velvet-wrapped package lay ten feet outside the fence. And the boys couldn't get it.

"Holy Mackerel! Holy Mackerel!" whispered the shorter boy. He sounded like someone was strangling the life out of him. "The MPs! They're running the fence! They'll see the package! We'll go to jail, Simon! They'll put us in jail, for sure! Come on, let's get out of here."

Simon stared at the package. The MPs were getting closer.

"I'm not leaving without it."

"Simon! Come on, Simon. It's not worth jail. They'll

lock us up, for sure." The shorter boy was really dancing a jig now. He was pulling on Simon like a kid asking for candy. And then he ran.

The MPs were getting closer. It was broad daylight and the velvet-wrapped package was right in their path. They would surely see it.

What was in that package? I had to know.

I crawled out of the hideout without making a noise. Then I sneaked up on the boy named Simon.

"I can get that for you," I said.

Simon spun around.

"I can fit under that hole. I've done it before."

"Then go!" he said.

"You'll show me what's inside," I said. It wasn't a question.

Simon didn't answer right away. The MPs were getting closer. "Go," he said, nodding his head.

I lay on my back and wriggled under the fence. Staying low, I grabbed the package and passed it to Simon through the hole. Then I dropped on my back again and made it under just as the MPs turned the corner.

One of the MPs was Sergeant McElway. As his horse trotted by, he tipped his helmet to me. "Miss Hazel," he said. Within a minute, the MPs were out of sight.

I turned around. Simon was gone.

I kicked a rock and then started for home. That's when I heard "Psst!" from inside the hideout. I looked over the oil drum and into the dimness.

Simon was inside, still holding the package.

17

Sign of the Rose

Simon sat cross-legged on the dirt floor.

"How did you know this hideout was here?" I asked.

"Everyone knows it's here," he answered. "Even the MPs."

"Oh." I didn't want my disappointment to show. "What are you staring at?" I asked.

"Nothin' much," he answered. "You just remind me of someone."

"Well, do it on your own time," I snapped. "It's buggy."

Simon laughed. "You see. That's just the kind of thing she would have said. I mean, exactly."

"So, *who*, for Pete's sake?"

"My kid sister, Alice. She would have gotten a kick out of you, for sure."

"She's not on the Hill?" I asked.

"Nah. She died. About two years ago. She got polio, and she didn't get better."

"Oh." I didn't know what to say. But when someone tells you that their kid sister died, you can't just say nothing. "So, what? Do I look like her?"

"Well, she was puny like you. And a pest like you. And what a mouth! She would talk your ear off!"

Now look. There were at least three insults right there. But when someone is talking about his kid sister who died, you're not supposed to get all mad at him, even if he does insult you. So I just said, "What did she talk about?"

"*Everything.*" He rolled his eyes. "She was really smart. I mean, way above average. Even smarter than me."

So he was insulting *and* conceited. Again, I had to let it go. The dead kid sister and all.

"You sure do remind me of her," he said. "She was really something."

That at least sounded nice. "I'm sorry," I said.

"Yeah, well," he said. "So you want to see what's inside?" He held up the velvet-wrapped package.

The hideout was dim, but not totally dark. There were spaces between the boards over our heads that let in light. Simon untied the string that held the bundle together.

The cloth fell away like water running over a stone.

In his hand were three glass tubes. Each one was about four inches long and had a coil of wires inside. They sort of looked like light bulbs, except that on one end of each tube there was a metal cap with prongs sticking out of it. Simon held one of the tubes up in the light. He stared at it, like it might talk to him.

"You don't know what this is," whispered Simon. "But I've been waiting three months for it."

"It's a vacuum tube," I said. Obviously. I picked up one of the tubes lying on the velvet. I shook it a little and heard a faint rattle inside. "This one's blown."

Simon stared at me like I had just sprouted a second head.

"How do you know about vacuum tubes?" he asked.

"Dunno. Just do. I guess I read about them somewhere. Or maybe I saw one in my dad's lab. He's a—" I wasn't supposed to say.

"I know, I know," said Simon. "He's an *engineer*."

"Yeah, right. An *engineer*." We both laughed.

"You're pretty smart," said Simon. As if *he* was already in college, or something!

"I'm in high school, you know," I said, miffed but trying not to sound it. "In fact, I could have gone to high school *last* year, but I declined."

This cracked Simon up. I mean, he rolled on the dirt floor.

"Quit it!" I said, punching him.

Simon straightened up, but he still had a smile on his face. "So, what do you think I'm gonna do with these three vacuum tubes?"

"You're not doing anything with the one that's dead," I said.

"Okay, okay. What am I gonna do with these *two* vacuum tubes?" His black eyes flashed. He was trying to get my goat.

The truth was, he had me. Electronics has never been my strong subject. I tried hard to think of ways I had seen vacuum tubes used. But I couldn't come up with a thing.

So I looked at the equation from the other side. Simon was a teenage boy. I asked myself, What are teenage boys interested in? Cars? Girls? Cowboys? Movies? Comic books? Pop music?

Music. Radio! Vacuum tubes could be used to transmit and receive radio frequency.

I looked at Simon. He looked just like a drawing in an old picture book of mine of Rumpelstiltskin just before the miller's daughter guesses his name. He thought he was the cat's meow!

"You're building a radio," I said, as if I had read about it in the *New York Times*.

Simon stopped smiling. He stuffed the tubes and the velvet into his jacket, bolted out of the hideout, and ran down the street.

Boys are strange, I thought.

I stood up. My legs felt cramped, and I was tired. Wait until I tell Eleanor this! I walked up the street slowly, thinking about everything that had happened. When I got to the pond, I heard running footsteps behind me. It was Simon.

"You might as well come with me," he said. "I swear, you're just like her. A real pest!"

He led me behind Central School to the western edge of the fence. One of the biggest holes on the Hill was there. All the kids knew about it and used it. Simon and I scooted under and then ducked into the woods. Deeper and deeper. Simon was watching for marks on the trees. Sometimes I could see them—small nicks in the bark—sometimes I couldn't. He moved so fast, I could tell we weren't lost. But I also knew I could never find my way out without his help.

And then he stopped, picked up a stick, and used it to knock six times on the trunk of a big pine tree. I heard a scuffling above, and a rope fell down. That's when I looked up.

Stuck in the boughs of the tree, almost completely out of sight, was a tree fort. Now *that's* a hideout, I thought. The fort was about the size of a really big closet, and from where I could see, it looked like it had four walls *and* a roof. The way in was through a hole cut in the floor. Not too pretty, but it worked.

Simon climbed up the knotted rope. I started to climb too. I was glad I was wearing blue jeans instead of a skirt, but I wished I'd had gloves on my hands. The rope was rough. It cut into my skin like the edge of a serrated knife.

When Simon reached the top, I felt a strong jerk on the rope that almost made me fall down. Then I heard Simon say, "Wait," to someone inside the tree fort. I scrambled to the top.

Inside was the boy who had run away from the MPs that afternoon.

"Are you off your rocker?" said the boy. He looked mad.

"No," said Simon. "She's in, if she wants to be. Do you want to be?" he asked, turning to me.

"In? Sure," I said.

"In means you can't tell anyone about this place or us or what we do here. Anyone! Do you get it?"

"Sure," I said. Another secret. I thought of my mother, and my heart sank. But I wanted to be in. Definitely. In.

"Simon! We gotta talk about this," said the boy. "You can't just decide—"

"She's in," said Simon. "What's your name?" he asked me.

"Hazel," I said.

"Hazel, this is Russell," said Simon. Russell looked like a geyser that was about to blow. But Simon didn't even notice.

I took a quick look around the fort. In one corner was a sort of crummy low table built out of scraps of wood. On top of the table were two wooden boxes, each one about the size of a bread box. The front panel on each box had a few switches and knobs, but none of them was labeled. Running out of the front of one of the boxes were two sets of headphones.

On the floor next to the table were piles and piles of magazines. I noticed the usual comic-book trash—*The Green Lantern* and *Dr. Fate* and *Johnny Thunder*. But there were also stacks of magazines called *QST* and *Radio News*. On top of the table, next to the boxes, was a dog-eared book. I could just make out the title: *The Radio Amateur's Handbook*. It looked like it had been read about a million times.

"Take a look at our setup," said Simon. He lifted the lid of one of the boxes on the table. At first, it looked like a bird's nest gone wrong. There was a tangle of wires, condensers, resistors, and sockets. But after looking at it closely for a minute or two, I could sort of follow the circuit. I could see where the dry-cell batteries hooked up, and I could follow the antenna out the back of the box and through the ceiling of the tree fort.

"That baby goes up forty feet," said Simon, watching my eyes follow the antenna wire out of sight.

"Where did you get all this stuff?" I asked.

"From the dump. You wouldn't believe what the army throws out," said Simon. "All the scrap wood and metal you could ask for. Wires! Mountains of 'em. I even picked up a busted old radio last winter. That's where we got the condensers and some of the resistors."

"Does it work?" I asked.

"Not yet," said Simon. "It's a three-tube set. And, as you pointed out, I've only got two working tubes. But I'm expecting another package from Aunt Esther. Maybe this week. Maybe next."

I looked carefully at the wooden boxes on the table. There were two. That's when I noticed—off to one side was a battered old microphone with its front piece missing. It looked like some sort of old war veteran standing at attention. "Hold on," I said. "You're receiving *and* sending signals?"

"Simon. . . ," said Russell. It sounded like a warning growl. "She's trouble."

Simon ignored Russell. "With a little fiddling, I should be able to reach the west coast. Who knows? Maybe even farther."

"But that's illegal," I said. "The President banned amateur radio for the duration. It's against the law."

Simon shrugged his shoulders. "As long as no one finds out, no one gets in trouble. Get it?"

"But someone could find out. Anyone could find out. Anyone who picks up your frequency."

"We'll change frequencies. We'll move the equipment. They won't be able to catch us."

"Simon, it isn't right."

Simon rolled his eyes. "Maybe it isn't right. But it isn't wrong, either. Haven't you ever heard of shades of gray? Come on. What's the big deal? We're not a security risk."

"But why are you doing it?" I asked.

He shrugged his shoulders. "If you have to ask, then you'll never know," he said. "Look. Have you ever talked to someone in Hong Kong? Have you ever had a friend in Saskatchewan? Try it. You'll get hooked."

I didn't *want* to get hooked. And I didn't want to break the law. But . . . it sounded like fun.

Simon put the tubes on the table and put the lid back on the receiver. Then we all climbed down the rope, and Russell threw it back up into the tree fort.

"How do you get up again?" I asked.

"Whoever gets here first has to climb the tree," explained Simon. "That's usually Russell. He can climb like a monkey."

We walked for almost five minutes. The sun was about to set. Suddenly, Simon and Russell stopped.

"This is where we split up," said Simon. "I'll show you the easy way out. Walk straight toward the sun for exactly one hundred yards. Then turn ninety degrees to your right. Follow that direction and you'll reach the edge of the woods behind the school."

"Okay," I said.

"So you're in, right?" he asked.

"Sure. I guess."

"Okay, then. We operate under the sign of the rose. Just like medieval secret societies. If you find a rose, it means there's a meeting. Otherwise, don't go to the tree fort, *no matter what.*"

"What do you mean, if I find a rose . . . ?" There were no roses on the Hill.

But the boys were gone.

I hurried toward the sun. In another few minutes it would set, and I'd have no way of finding my way out of the woods. Soon I was diving under the fence behind the school.

I started for home, but stopped. I ended up walking around and around the pond. Thinking.

It was a question of loyalty, wasn't it? And my loyalties were pretty clear cut, weren't they? My parents? Definitely. FDR? Absolutely. My friends? Of course. But who came first? Parents before friends? Old friends before new friends? And FDR before all? It was a puzzle, and I walked around and around and around the pond, trying to make the pieces fit.

And when I couldn't make it all work out, I started to wonder if in was better than out. Or just a whole mess of trouble.

18

Pretty Neat

With Eleanor's help, I finished the socks. They weren't perfect, but they weren't a total disgrace. It was more than I had hoped for. Eleanor said they were *fabulous*, which was her new movie-star word. Whenever she said it, it sounded like this: *faaaaa*-bulous.

I couldn't help it. I felt guilty around Eleanor. I had a secret—and it was a walloping one. But I couldn't talk to her about it. I couldn't talk to anyone about it.

I was all mixed up. The radio was illegal. The President had said that all amateur radio transmissions must stop for the duration. And I trusted FDR more than any person on earth, except my own mom and dad. FDR was a great man and a great leader. He was courageous and honest, and if he said that amateur radio had to stop, then he must have a pretty good reason.

National security. That's what FDR said.

But what did that mean? To me, national security meant not telling our enemies anything that would help them win the war. Like how many planes we were building in our factories. Or where we planned to attack next.

I could understand that. I didn't want to give the enemy an advantage. There was a poster in the commissary that showed two women working in a factory. One was whispering to the other, and you could see, in the background, Nazi planes bombing an American warship. The caption read, "Loose lips sink ships. Button up and bring our boys home!"

But *we* didn't work in a wartime factory. We didn't know anything important. We were just kids stuck in the middle of the desert who wanted to have a little fun. Simon wasn't a spy. He wasn't going to give away important security information to the enemy. Why wasn't it okay for him to use the radio he had built himself?

Sometimes I wanted to talk to Eleanor about all this. But mostly, I wanted to talk to my mom. I wanted to tell her all about Simon and the tree fort and the radio. I wanted her to tell me what I should do.

But if I talked to my mom then the secret would be out. And that's the problem with secrets. Once they're out, there's no way to get them back in.

So I buttoned up. And sat tight.

A week passed, then two. I started to think I had dreamed the whole thing.

Then one afternoon, I was sitting with Eleanor and Gemma in our classroom. It was lunchtime. Everyone else had gone home to eat lunch, but Eleanor and Gemma and I were having a special lunch meeting because of the play that the high school kids were putting on. The three of us were responsible for making the costumes, which is one of those lousy jobs that the older kids always give to the seventh graders.

The whole point of the lunch meeting that day was to make a list of the costumes we needed. But as soon as we sat down, we started talking, of course, about the movie we'd seen last night in Theater No. 2. It was *The Fighting Sullivans*, and it was the true story of five brothers who all died in the war in the Pacific. The three of us had cried our eyes out last night, and we just couldn't stop talking about it today.

I reached into my lunch sack and felt a sharp stab.

"Ow!" I exclaimed, as I pulled out my hand. A drop of blood hung on my fingertip. I looked inside the bag. There was a dried rose next to my egg salad sandwich. The petals were stiff and dull, but the thorns were as sharp as ever.

"What is it?" asked Eleanor, leaning over to peer into my sack.

"Nothing," I said, quickly closing my bag. "My mother put a fork in my bag by mistake." I carefully pulled out my sandwich and began to wolf it down.

Eleanor and Gemma kept talking, but I wasn't listening.

The sign of the rose! Just like medieval secret societies. It meant there was a meeting at the tree fort. Should I go right away? Or was it okay to wait until school was over?

A hundred thoughts rushed through my mind. Maybe Simon had managed to get the extra tubes he needed. Or maybe the MPs had discovered the radio.

Eleanor nudged me.

"Is that okay with you?" she asked.

I hadn't heard a word. "Sorry. What?" My mouth was full of egg salad.

"We're going to try to rummage up scrap fabric today. After school. Okay?"

"Oh," I said, faking disappointment. "I can't. I promised my mom I'd do some chores around the house today. I have to clean all the windows and—the stove. I have to clean the stove. It's a real mess. I promised her. Right after school."

"Why doesn't your mom just get a maid, like all the other moms?" asked Gemma, a little annoyed.

"Well, my mom doesn't work, so the army won't give her a maid."

"That's not true," said Gemma. "Even if you don't work, you can have a maid. You just don't get as many days as the moms who work. Tell your mom. The maids are free."

"I think my mom kind of likes being in charge of her own house. I don't think she'd want a maid, even for free."

"Your mom's kind of eccentric, isn't she?" asked Gemma.

"No, she's not!" I said.

"She's just sort of strange, that's all. I mean, she's *always* home. Always."

"She is *not!*' I interrupted. "She goes out sometimes."

"She never comes to our house," said Gemma. "And my mom invites her all the time. I overheard my mom talking, and she said that your mom has agoraphobia."

I could feel steam coming out of my ears. "*Your* mom," I started to say.

"Oh, for Pete's sake, cut it out," said Eleanor. "I don't

even know what agoraphobia is, and I don't care. Let's talk about the costumes, instead. Here's an idea: Gemma and I will help with the windows and the stove. It can't take that long with three of us working. Then we'll still have time to start on the costumes."

"Oh, I don't think so," I said. "I think my mom wants me to do the work myself. She says hard work builds character."

"You see! That's exactly what I'm talking about," said Gemma. "Any other mother would . . . "

"Okay, okay," said Eleanor. "Gemma and I will go to Gemma's house. You come over when you're finished with your chores. How's that?"

"That's a good plan," I said.

Keeping a secret meant a lot more than just keeping my mouth shut.

After school, Eleanor and Gemma and I walked together as far as my apartment. Then the two of them headed on to Gemma's.

I stood on the steps for a minute, then I doubled back to the school and crawled under the fence. Snow crept into my collar as I squirmed under, and I shivered as I stood and looked at the woods. I thought about running back to the house to put on my blue jeans. I had worn my usual school outfit that day: a wool skirt and sweater, ankle socks, and saddle shoes. Who knew I'd be tramping through the woods? My legs missed the warmth of thick denim. But if I went to the house, my mom might be sitting in her pajamas, staring out the window or reading a newspaper from six months ago. I didn't want to see that. Not right now.

So I decided to just keep going. But a thought occurred to me suddenly: How would I find my way to the tree fort? I couldn't just walk into the woods and hope to stumble on it. The woods were deep, and the tree fort was well hidden.

That's when I noticed the tracks. They led straight into the woods. I began to follow them. But after a few minutes, the tracks were joined by others. They began to run in all different directions, crisscrossing each other until it was impossible to tell where they led.

I walked first this way, then that, until I stood still, not knowing which way to turn. Suddenly, a snowball hit me on the shoulder. I spun around. There was the rope. I climbed up quickly.

At the top, Simon was grinning. "You'll have to learn your own way to the fort," he said. "We usually cover our tracks with a pine branch. Next time, I'll show you how."

Russell was sitting next to the radio table with a pair of headphones on. He didn't say hello.

Nuts to you, too, I thought to myself.

I suddenly realized how cold I was. My feet were wet and my coat was soaked through. I felt my teeth chatter, like someone was playing castanets in my skull.

"We have blankets," said Simon, noticing my shaking hands. "And hot coffee." He indicated some rumpled army-issue blankets in the corner and a Captain Midnight thermos on the floor—the gift from Aunt Esther!

I took off my coat and wrapped a scratchy wool blanket around me. It smelled of moth balls, but made me feel warmer.

"What's up?" I asked Simon. "Why the meeting?"

Simon was already back at the radio table with the other pair of headphones around his neck. He had a screwdriver in his hands, and he was tinkering with the inside of the receiver. "I got another birthday present," he said. "This time from my Uncle Mel." Simon gave Russell a nudge. "Hey, Russell. Give her a turn with the headphones."

"Why should I?" snarled Russell.

"'Cause she's the one who went under the fence to get the tubes," hissed Simon. "*Remember?*"

Russell snapped the headphones off his ears and tossed them at me. I sat down on the floor next to Simon and put the headphones on. Russell sulked in a corner with the latest issue of *QST*.

The receiver was opened up, and I could see that all three tubes were in their sockets. Simon tightened something inside the box. Then he put down the screwdriver and flipped a switch. A loud hum buzzed in my ears. Simon grunted and flipped the switch off. The buzzing stopped. Then he leaned over to look at the guts of the box. He pulled out one of the tubes and flipped the switch again. The hum was much lower.

"Heater-to-cathode leakage," he muttered. He handed the bum tube to me, picked up another tube, and plugged it into the socket. Then he flipped the switch. Nothing happened.

"Dead," said Simon. Another tube was tossed my way. Simon reached for the last tube and plugged it in. The same loud hum came through the headphones.

"What the devil . . . ?" he cursed. He thought for a minute. I kept my trap shut. Simon's one of those people, you just don't interrupt them when they're thinking. The hum through the headphones was loud, like a swarm of locusts surrounding the tree fort.

All of a sudden, Simon reached his hand into the receiver and held it near the tube. The hum grew even louder. When he moved his hand away, the hum was a little quieter. Simon flipped off the power switch.

"Okay. Now I got ya," he said. He rummaged through a crate that was filled with scraps of metal. He pulled out something that looked like part of a coffee can. He grabbed a hammer and a pair of pliers and started banging and twisting the metal. Then he carefully put it in the receiver box so that it shielded the tube.

Simon flipped the power switch again. The hum was almost gone.

"Okay," I heard him say, mostly to himself. "It's been a while. Let's see if I remember . . ." He put his hand on one of the knobs and started to turn it. "Move the regen control slowly until the set starts to oscillate. Hold it there, then tune . . ."

A couple of minutes passed. There was a lot of noise in the headphones—hissing and crackling—but no voices. I started to get a headache, so I took off the headphones to give my ears a break.

Suddenly, a giant smile broke out on Simon's face. He flipped a switch on the transmitter, turned a knob, and leaned into the microphone.

"N3MK N3MK from K3JD K3JD from . . . from . . ." Simon halted. He couldn't give his real location. None of us was allowed to even say the name of the town out loud. But Simon was a quick thinker. "From Las Palomas, Mexico. Your RST is 579. My name is Simon. Simon. So how do you copy? N3MK from K3JD. Go ahead."

As soon as Simon started talking, Russell streaked over to the radio table and grabbed the headphones that I'd put down. He was in such a hurry to get them on his head that he got his left arm all tangled up in the cord.

"Holy Toledo," I heard him whisper. "We did it. We really did it."

Simon was quiet for a moment. He was concentrating so hard that his forehead bunched up and his eyebrows flew up like arrows shot into the sky.

"*Hola*, Brian!" continued Simon. "I've got some friends who would like to say hello to you. Can you hold?"

Simon took off his headphones and put them on my head. Then he pushed the microphone in my direction. "We've got Brian in Guadalajara."

The microphone was right in front of me. Speaking into it was against the law. But there was a person on the other end who was a thousand miles away. We were so cut off on the Hill. How could this have anything to do with national security?

"How's the weather down there?" I shouted. Not exactly brilliant, but I really wanted to know. I was talking to someone who was off the Hill! I was talking to someone who was a thousand miles away! I was talking to someone I had never met and would never see in my whole life. Someone from a different world.

By the time I handed the headphones back to Simon, my heart was pounding and my palms were sweaty.

"Pretty neat, huh?" said Simon.

I had to admit it was pretty neat.

19

Hotspots

Russell didn't like me and I didn't like him and that was fine. But Simon—finding Simon was like finding a brother I'd never known I had. After two weeks, I felt like I'd known him my whole life.

The three of us sneaked off to the radio every chance we got. Sneaking meant lying—sometimes to my mom, sometimes to Eleanor. With my mom, I used the excuse of studying at a friend's house. With Eleanor, I decided the safest story was sickness. I said I was sick. I said my mom was sick. Sometimes I said both of us were sick. Nobody double-checks on sickness.

The radio was like a magic door. Each time we opened it, we found ourselves in a strange, new place. We talked to people in Tijuana and Moose Jaw and Walla Walla. Simon was constantly fiddling with the guts, adding new parts, and fine-tuning the controls so that we could go farther. Who knew? Someday we might be able to reach South America! The thought was thrilling enough to keep me coming back.

One afternoon about a month after I met Simon, we were all at the tree fort. Simon had found an old radio at the dump, and he was ripping it apart. Russell was reading a

Captain Marvel comic book, and I was copying an English composition that I had to hand in the next day. It was an essay called, "What It Means to Be an American." But while I was copying, I was thinking. And since I was thinking, I started talking.

"Hey, Simon," I said. "Do you know who Uncle Nick *really* is?" Uncle Nick was this old fizzler on the Hill. The grownups called him Nicholas Baker and the kids all called him Uncle Nick, but the army couldn't fool me. I knew he was Niels Bohr, the world's greatest atomic scientist, all the way from Denmark. The Nazis had taken over Denmark the same way they'd taken over most of Europe. But Niels Bohr had escaped in the night. Escaped, and then turned up here.

"Yep," said Simon. He didn't even look up, the stinker.

"Who? Who is he?" asked Russell.

"How do you know?" I asked, ignoring Russell.

"Hazel. Anyone with half a brain knows who Uncle Nick really is."

That shut Russell up.

"Well, what do you think of that?" I asked.

He shrugged his shoulders and kept ripping wires out of the old radio.

"You've never wondered why Uncle Nick is here?" I said.

Simon shrugged his shoulders again.

"The thought has never crossed your mind that Uncle Nick is the key to the mystery? Your puny little brain has never wondered . . ."

"Aw, quit it, would ya?" interrupted Simon. "You're just trying to be a pest."

"You know, you're a waste of space," I said. "All that brain power and not an ounce of curiosity. You'll never get anywhere worth going."

Simon was holding a screwdriver, and he looked like he wanted to bean me. "As long as I don't have to go anywhere with you," he muttered.

"Just admit it," I said. "Admit you can't figure out what the gadget is. Say, 'I am too stupid to solve the mystery of the gadget.' And I'll shut up."

"Say it, Simon," growled Russell, his nose buried in his comic book. "For God's sake, just say it!"

But Simon couldn't. He was like me. He wanted to know. And I knew he wanted to know. But he didn't want me to know that he wanted to know. Boys! They're just more trouble than they're worth.

"Look. It's obvious," I said. "They're working on the subatomic structure of *something*," I said. "They've got some kind of radioactive reaction going on in there. I've heard my dad say that the Tech Area is so hot it could thaw the North Pole in January. Hot means radioactive. And every time the town fire alarm goes off, my dad looks like a ghost until he hears the all clear for the Tech Area."

"It's a chain reaction," said Simon thoughtfully. "You can bet that. They're working on a sustained nuclear reaction."

I nodded my head. "Fermi's work," I said. "But what are they doing with it? They're taking the theory of a chain reaction and turning it into something. Something that will end the war."

"I know what the gadget is," said Russell. We stared at him. "I mean it! I really do. I overheard a couple of soldiers talking at the PX. It's a gun. A super gun that shoots atoms instead of bullets. The atoms can burn a hole right through you, even miles away. It's a super atom gun."

"It's not a gun," I said. "My dad would never make a gun."

"Why not?" asked Russell. "Doesn't he want the war to end?"

"Of course he does, you idiot. But he would never make a stupid gun. My dad hates guns."

"Oh, that's real logical. He'll make a submarine that can kill people, but he won't make a gun. What did you think—that we were going to end the war without killing anyone? Girls are so dumb!"

"I am not dumb! And my dad would never make anything as . . . *unimaginative* as a gun. There *is* a difference between a submarine and a gun. A big difference. A submarine can be used for other things, peaceful things, after the war. But a gun is just a gun. It can't do anything except kill."

"Energy," said Simon. "It's a nearly limitless supply of energy."

"That's what I'm thinking," I said, turning my back on Russell. "Atomic energy. But for what? What are they trying to power? Not a submarine, like everyone says. A submarine isn't going to win the war."

"Maybe ships," said Simon. "Imagine a whole fleet of ships that can travel a hundred times faster and a thousand times farther. That could win the war."

"Ships aren't going to beat the Nazis. Germany is practically landlocked."

"Maybe it's not the Germans we're trying to beat."

"What do you mean?" I said. "Of course it's the Germans we're trying to beat."

"Nah. The Krauts are already on the run," said Simon. "Look at the way we bombed Hamburg. And now the Brits are bombing Berlin. There won't be anything left of Berlin by the spring. The Nazis will surrender and that will be that."

Hamburg. My stomach did a somersault. I couldn't even hear the word without feeling like I was going to throw up.

"The Nazis are history," said Simon. "But the Japs! That's another story. They'll never surrender. Not until the last one is dead in the jungle. They're the ones we have to beat."

Japan. Japan was even farther away than Europe, and the fighting there was twice as bloody. Hand-to-hand combat. Kamikaze attacks. Mrs. Talbot had a brother over there. Eleanor and I read his letters in secret. "They just won't give up," he wrote, after the battle at Guadalcanal. "Even if you're holding a gun to their heads, they just won't give up. It's like they're not even human."

There was something scary about the Japanese, even scarier than the Nazis. The Pacific was the hotspot. If you had a son, or a brother, or a sweetheart going off to war, you sure hoped he was going anywhere in Europe and not to fight the bloody Japs on those godforsaken islands. But I still couldn't believe that a ship, even an atomic one, was going to win the war.

"What else besides ships?" I asked. "What about airplanes? What about . . . a rocket? Why not an atomic rocket?"

Russell laughed. "Flash Gordon to the rescue!" He made a loud explosion sound and pretended his hand was a rocket taking off. What a moron!

"Do you think that's what it is?" I asked Simon. "An atomic rocket?"

"Maybe," he said. "Maybe a rocket that could carry bombs. That would be something the world has never seen."

"I hope that's what it is," said Russell. "I hope we wipe every Jap off the map." Russell had a cousin who was killed at Bataan. He hated the Japanese, all of them.

I heard my mother's voice in my ear. I heard her words—simple and true. But how was I supposed to tell Russell that the Japanese were people too? How was I supposed to tell him that little babies—even Japanese babies—aren't supposed to die?

I could see the hatred in Russell's eyes. His cousin had been like a brother to him.

I decided to keep my mouth shut. But in my mind, I had a new picture. A picture of something beautiful and brilliant flying into outer space. Flying on the power of an atom.

20

A Voice in the Night

It was the ides of March and cold. The wind that blew down from the mountains sliced my face whenever I stepped outside, especially at night. And nighttime was when we met at the tree fort.

We'd been transmitting for almost two months, and the MPs still hadn't caught us. Not that they weren't trying. First there was an article in the *Bulletin* listing all the terrible things that would happen to anyone found operating an illegal radio. Going to jail was at the top of the list. Then notices were posted around town with FDR's orders forbidding amateur broadcasting during the war. Then the MPs started questioning parents. They even raided the woods a couple of times.

Simon's theory was, as long as we kept moving the radio every few days, they'd never be able to track us down.

At first I was really scared of getting caught. I had terrible nightmares about going to jail or being executed by a firing squad for treason.

But after a while, I figured Simon was right. If they hadn't caught us by now, they never would. We were extra careful about our secret meetings. We met in the middle of the night, and we always covered our tracks.

But everything changed one night in the middle of March. It was late, past midnight, the safest time for sending signals. We had scheduled a radio contact with a boy in Mexico City, a risky thing to do because it involved giving out our frequency and a specific time when we would be broadcasting. If the MPs were listening, they could track us.

Simon was working the dial, and I was listening in. Russell was right at Simon's elbow, waiting his turn. We heard nothing but static and then some music and then more static. All of a sudden a signal came in so clear that it made Simon jump for the volume control. It was a voice, and it sounded like it was in the next room. But it wasn't speaking English.

"Holy Toledo!" said Simon, fine-tuning with the knob.

It was the clearest signal we'd ever received on the radio. Simon and I listened carefully. I looked at his face. I could tell he didn't understand a word. Simon slipped off his headphones so they hung around his neck and motioned for me to do the same.

"What kind of language is that?" asked Simon.

"Russian," I said.

"Russian?" asked Simon. "You know Russian?"

"Some. My mother's grandmother was from Russia. She lived with my grandparents in Nebraska, but she visited us every summer when I was little."

"I can't believe we reached Russia!" said Russell. "That's got to be two thousand miles away!" He reached for the headphones. "Let me listen!"

"We didn't reach Russia, knucklehead," said Simon. "That signal is just around the corner." He pushed away Russell's waving hand and put his headphones back on. I put mine on, too.

The person was talking slowly. There was absolutely no expression in his voice. It sounded like he was reading a grocery list. I was used to my great-grandmother's fury of language. She spoke Russian as if the words were on fire.

I couldn't understand much. I recognized some numbers. And then something about an egg. An egg? I thought that's what the voice had said. And then the speaker stopped, and the signal turned to static.

Simon and I took off our headphones.

"Did you lose it?" asked Russell. "Is the signal gone?"

"Yeah," said Simon.

"Well, give me a turn," said Russell. "Maybe I can still reach Mexico City."

Simon gave up his seat in front of the microphone, and Russell put on the headphones. Simon sat cross-legged on the floor on the other side of the tree fort. I sat down next to him and pulled a blanket around my shoulders.

"What was he talking about?" asked Simon.

"I couldn't get much," I said. "I heard some numbers. And something about an egg, I think. And then, I don't know. It just didn't make any sense."

"I wonder who he was talking to. How come we never heard the other person?" Simon was puzzling. His forehead wrinkled up.

"And where was he broadcasting from?" I asked. "The

only people who can send signals within a hundred miles of here are the army. And they're not broadcasting in Russian."

"Are you sure it was Russian?" asked Simon.

I nodded my head.

There was another long pause. I kept stealing looks at Simon, but he just stared at the floor with his face all bunched up.

"You're thinking what I'm thinking, aren't you?" I said.

"Depends what you're thinking," said Simon. "I'm not a mind reader!"

Simon sure could be a pain in the neck sometimes.

"Well, why don't you tell me what you're thinking and I'll tell you if it's the same thing I'm thinking," I said. I could be a pain in the neck, too.

"Not on your life! You first."

"Not on your life!" We sat there, not talking to each other for a whole minute. Why do boys have to be so horrible?

"I'm thinking that we just heard a spy on the radio!" I said. "What do you think of that?"

"I think you read too many dime-store novels."

"There's no other explanation," I said. "There's a spy on the Hill."

"You're nuts!" Simon said.

"Why? Why is that so crazy? Do you think we're the only ones who want to know about the gadget? It makes sense. There's a spy on the Hill, sending information back to the Russians!"

"First of all, Miss Paranoid," said Simon. "The Russians are our allies. Remember? They're fighting on the same side as us. And second of all, we know everyone on the Hill. How could a spy be someone we know?"

"That's a dumb argument," I said. "Just because the Russians are fighting with us doesn't mean we trust them. I mean, do you trust Joseph Stalin? Do you think FDR trusts Joseph Stalin? Come on, Simon. There's a war going on. And for your information, there are spies all over the country."

"No. I don't believe it. There's got to be another explanation."

Just then Russell took off his headphones.

"Zip," said Russell. He turned off the radio. "What are you guys talking about?"

"Nothing," said Simon. "Let's get cracking. We need to move the radio tonight."

"But we just moved it yesterday," groaned Russell.

"Doesn't matter," replied Simon, starting to gather spare cables and the tool box. "We're moving again."

Russell was used to following Simon's orders. He started to disconnect the radio.

Simon turned to me and whispered, "Let's keep this between the two of us, okay?"

I nodded yes, but I began to look at Simon in a different way. What was he afraid of? What was he hiding? Suddenly, I wasn't so sure who I could trust.

21

Sleeping Giants

I dreamed I was being chased through the woods. I ran faster than I've ever run in my life, leaping over fallen tree trunks and rocks. It was almost like flying. But still I could hear the pounding footsteps behind me, sometimes farther, sometimes closer.

Suddenly, I was racing down the hallway of Central School, and this time, I was the one doing the chasing. Up ahead was a shadowy figure, dressed in a gray overcoat and hat, just like Dick Tracy. It was the spy, and I had him cornered. He darted into Mrs. Burrows's classroom, and I followed. There was no way out. He turned to face me.

It was Simon.

"How could you do this?" I asked. He was my friend, and he had lied to me. I felt like a bug that had been stepped on.

Then I noticed that Simon was holding an egg. An evil smile crept over his face.

"Poison," he said and threw the egg at me. It hit me in the head, and I knew I was going to die.

That's when I woke up.

I lay in bed, afraid to move. My hair was plastered to

my cheeks and the back of my neck. My flannel night-gown was drenched in sweat. When I tried to peel the sticky layer away from my skin, I noticed that my hands were shaking.

I crawled to the window next to my bed and shoved it open. Cold March air rushed into the room like water breaking over a dam. Within seconds my damp body began to shiver, and I dived under my blanket, burning and freezing at the same time.

Sometimes, dreams are so real that even after you wake up it's hard to believe they didn't happen. I *knew* Simon wasn't the spy. He had been sitting right next to me when we heard the spy talking on the radio. My *head* knew that he wasn't the spy. But my *heart* felt like he was. Instead of friendship, I felt treachery. Why?

I tried to think of everything I knew about Simon and was surprised to realize just how little it was. I knew he was brave and loyal and smart. I knew he was sarcastic and selfish and full of himself. I knew that back home, he loved going to Yankees games. Of course, there was no baseball here. I knew that he had a few trophies from state and national science competitions, but there were no competitions like that on the Hill. I knew that he missed his two best friends from back home. He wrote letters to them all the time, but a lot of the letters were returned by the censor. Too descriptive. Too informative.

All of a sudden, I had a different picture of Simon. He had always seemed so big to me, larger than life, someone who had everything—brains and guts and determination.

But now I saw him as someone who had lost everything. All the things that mattered to him.

This year, Simon was a senior. But when he graduated, there would be no yearbook or end-of-the-year ceremony. There was no marching band or school newspaper or honors society at our school. No clubs, no pep squad. No prom queen or valedictorian.

For the kids on the Hill, there was just school and running wild.

Which was enough for me. But maybe it wasn't for him. Maybe a boy like him wanted more than what you could find on the Hill.

And then I got to thinking that maybe that was the reason he cared so much about his dumb old radio. It was more to him than just a way to pass the time. It was his only way to get away from the Hill, as far away as he needed to go.

And that's when I realized why Simon couldn't let on that the voice on the radio might belong to a spy. Because he knew I would go to the MPs. There was no other way. I couldn't help hide a spy with the war going on and all. And once I went to the MPs, the radio would be confiscated. And that would be just the beginning.

I felt the way I do when I play chess and suddenly I see the way the game is going to play out: The pawn will capture the rook, the bishop will capture the pawn, and the king will be left in checkmate. In some games of chess, you reach a point where the outcome becomes inevitable. That's what would happen if Simon admitted to me that the voice on the radio might belong to a spy. The game would play out to its inevitable end.

Have you ever heard the expression *caught between a rock and a hard place*? That's what I felt like. On one side of me was Simon, my friend. On the other side was FDR, the president. They both deserved my loyalty. But I couldn't be loyal to both.

What if I didn't tell? Would it be so bad? It's not like I knew the spy's name or where he was. I hardly had anything to tell. Just that I heard a voice speaking Russian. Was that little bit of information worth losing the radio? Worth hurting Simon?

That's when I heard a chair scrape in the living room.

I crept out of bed and down the hallway barefoot. My mother was sitting in the living room. She had turned the large armchair to face the window that overlooked the Sangre de Cristo mountains. In the moonlight, they looked like giant sleeping bears, heaped in a pile, their delicate spines pointing to the sky. My mother sat in the armchair with a red wool shawl wrapped around her shoulders. Her legs were tucked under her, and her long hair was draped over the back of the chair.

I stood next to the chair. I knew she could see me, but she didn't move.

"Mom?" There was so much I wanted to say. About the radio and sneaking around and pretending to be someone I'm not and all the lies, little and big, that had crept into my life since coming to the Hill. But there were so many words, it would take so many words just to say that, and I couldn't find the one word to go first.

"Mom?"

"Hmmm?" My mother continued to look at the mountains, as if we met like this every night.

"Oh, Mom," I whispered. "I've been telling lies!"

She looked at me. "You must be cold then," she said. "Come here." And she opened up the shawl like an eagle spreading its wings, and I crawled inside that warm cocoon and buried myself in her familiar smell.

When I could talk, I began. "I don't know what to do. You see, there's this friend of mine. And I might have to rat on him. I don't want to. I want to be a good friend. But what he's doing is wrong. And I don't know what to do about it."

My mother used her fingers to comb my tangled hair. Her hands moved so slowly that it didn't hurt. Even when she came to a snarl, she worked so gently that the snarl seemed to undo itself without a single tug.

"Have you asked yourself the important questions?" she asked. "Who will be helped and who will be hurt?"

"I've tried, but it doesn't help. You see, someone I know will be hurt very much. And a lot of people I don't know will be helped, maybe. But maybe not."

"Oh, Hazel. These answers are never simple. How do you weigh a person's pain? How do you measure the help you give? Let's just say it's a simple mathematical equation. One person harmed, many people saved. That seems simple, doesn't it? But what if the harm to the one is so great that it outweighs all the help you give to the many?

And what if you believe—some people do—that one life is worth more than another? How does that change the equation? Is the life of a good person worth the lives of two bad people? Is the life of a person with white skin worth the lives of two people with yellow skin? With so many variables, it's very hard to do the math."

"I can't figure it out," I said. "I can't. Maybe . . . maybe the best thing is to do nothing."

"Maybe. I have a feeling you won't be happy with that."

We sat in silence for several minutes. Dawn broke behind the Sangre de Cristos. The sleeping giants turned purple, then yellow. I could have sworn they moved, but my eyes were tired and liable to play tricks. It was my mother who finally spoke.

"You can puzzle and figure and calculate all you want. But in the end, Hazel, the answer will come, not from your head, but from your heart. You have a voice inside you. A voice that knows the answer to every question. It's hard to hear, I know. Especially here. There's something about this place that seems to drown out the voices inside us. But listen. Listen. And you'll know what to do."

The touch of my mother's hand, the rise and fall of her voice, were so comforting, I thought I would fall asleep right there on her lap. I felt warm and safe. The problems of the world, Simon's problems, FDR's problems, the problems of faceless men fighting thousands of miles away, all seemed indistinct and insignificant. The world was goldenrod yellow and as quiet as a frozen lake.

My mother leaned forward, burying her face in the

warm crook of my neck, like a horse nuzzling for a hidden sugar cube. She whispered, "If it makes you feel any better, I've been telling lies, too."

"You?"

My mom nodded her head. "What's worse, I've been unfaithful to your father."

"Unfaithful?"

"In the worst possible way." She held me tightly, as if she was afraid I might get away. "The whole time he's been working so hard to succeed, *I've been hoping that he fails.* Can you imagine how horrible that is? To wish failure for the person you love most in the world? I feel like the most terrible traitor!"

"Why, Mom?" I was confused. "Why do you want dad to fail? Don't you want the war to end?"

My mom's voice sounded like a worn-down needle scratching on an old phonograph record. "Oh, I can't bear it. Some days, I think I'll be torn in two."

We didn't say anything more that night. It was just too hard.

22

Out

When I woke up, I was in my own bed, and my voice had spoken to me.

I pulled on my snow boots and heavy coat, and I went to find Simon.

I had never been to Simon's house. That was strictly against club rules. But I knew he lived in McKeeville, the part of town that was nothing but rows and rows of identical one-story houses. There's a story around town that one of the McKeeville moms planted red geraniums outside her front door because otherwise she couldn't tell which house was hers, and she was tired of getting lost every time she went to the laundry. I don't know if the story is true, but it sure could have been. Whenever I'm in McKeeville, I start to feel like I'm in a house of mirrors. Everywhere you look you see the same house, over and over, in rows that just go on forever.

As I walked down one street, I noticed that some of the houses had blue-star banners hanging in their windows. I'd almost forgotten about those. None of the scientists were old enough to have sons fighting overseas. Here in McKeeville, a lot of the dads were workmen on the Hill, and they had boys who were old enough to be drafted.

I walked down another street, and then another, looking for—I don't know what. There was no sign pointing me in the right direction. I would have to ask for help. I went up to one of the houses and knocked. Just as I did, I noticed the gold-star banner in the window. I had to fight the urge to run. How could I knock on the door of a gold-star mother?

The door opened. A woman wearing a housedress and slippers stood there. She was wiping her floury hands on her apron. The smell of bread came from her kitchen.

It was Mrs. Sanchez. She was a cook at Fuller Lodge. Her only son Pablo was a soldier fighting in Europe. I had heard her talking with pride about him one day on the porch of Fuller Lodge.

"Mrs. Sanchez . . ." I faltered. "I was wondering . . . can you tell me where Simon Rabinov lives? I know it's around here, but I don't know the exact house."

Mrs. Sanchez shook her head and apologized. Her apology sounded very formal and sad with her heavy Spanish accent.

"I'm sorry," I said. "I'm so sorry . . ." I turned and ran back into the street.

I knocked on more doors. It took about an hour, but I finally found the right house. I was hoping it would be Simon who answered the door, because if it was his mom, I might lose my nerve. "Simon," I practiced under my breath, "I know you're not going to like what I have to say . . ."

But when the door flew open and there was Simon, I

blurted out, "You look terrible!" He had dark circles under his eyes, and his hair pointed every way but down.

Simon scowled. "You're breaking club rules," he said. "I can't let you in."

I pushed my way past him, and he let me get away with it.

"Sometimes you act like you're Eleanor Roosevelt, you know that?"

He closed the door, and I took a deep breath. "I'm going this morning to tell the army about the voice we heard on the radio. And that's *all* I'm going to tell."

"You don't think they might ask you a few questions, like where's the radio? Who built it? How long has this been going on?"

"They can ask, but I won't answer. Even," my lip trembled a little, "even if they torture me!"

"Oh, for crying out loud, Hazel. Sometimes you are such a *kid*! We're not talking about the SS. The army's not going to torture you. But they'll keep after you until you tell them everything. And you will. In the end, you'll tell all about the radio and that will be the end of it."

Simon kicked the sofa and then picked up a book that was lying on the coffee table and threw it across the room. It slammed into the wall and fell in a heap on the floor, the pages all crumpled. I'd never seen Simon so angry.

"If Alice was here," I said, "she'd want you to tell the army."

"Well she's *not*! You get it? She's not here. It's just me.

All alone. Stuck on top of this damn hill forever. And now the only thing that makes this stinking place bearable—*the only thing*—I'm going to lose that, too. Because you want to be some kind of a war hero. Like it makes any difference at all!"

Simon was pacing back and forth in the room, kicking anything that fell in his path.

"I'm not going to let you do it!" he yelled. "Do you hear me! I'm not going to let you ruin everything! I'll keep your mouth shut, so help me God!"

He lunged forward and tried to grab my arms. Before I knew what I was doing I bit him. I'm pretty ashamed of that, but really, there was no time to think. Anyway, it sure stopped him dead in his tracks. He stood there without moving, looking at the bloody tooth marks I had left on his arm. Neither of us said anything for about a minute.

"I'm sorry," I said. "I didn't mean, I mean, I didn't mean to break the skin."

He waved my apology away. "'S'okay," he said. "My fault."

I could taste the blood in my mouth, and it made me feel a little queasy. I sat down on the couch. Simon sat down next to me, still staring at the tooth marks.

"The only other person who ever bit me was Alice," he said. "Deserved it then, too."

"You know, you'll have to go see Dr. Coles about that," I said. "Human bites are even worse than dog bites. You can get really sick from them."

"Yeah, I know. I'll go see Dr. Coles after I talk to the army."

"No, I should be the one who talks to them. I won't get in nearly as much trouble as you. I mean, look at me. I'm just a girl. What's the worst they could do to me?"

"Maybe you're right," he said. He sat thinking for a while. "But, but could you give me a little time? Just a little? Wait two days, maybe? One day, even?"

"What's the point?"

"I just want a couple more tries. Just to see how far I can go. I won't transmit. I promise! I'll just receive."

I shook my head no.

"Oh, come on!' he said. "Today, tomorrow? What's the diff? The army will know soon enough. Give me the weekend. Just until Monday. Come on, Hazel! It won't kill you."

I looked at Simon. The bite on his arm looked nasty. It was already swelling into a ring of little welts. There were three drops of blood on his shirt. Somehow, they looked festive.

"All right. Three days. That's it! At noon on Monday, I'm going to tell the head of security. But I promise I won't tell him about you or Russell. Just about the spy. Just about what we heard."

"Thanks," said Simon.

I spent the rest of the day at home. I told Eleanor I had a head cold and I didn't want to expose her to it. My mom spent the whole day on the couch in the living room reading old newspapers and drinking cup after cup of tea. She never changed out of her pajamas.

Sometime in the afternoon, a thought occurred to me. I jumped out of bed and tugged on my boots and coat.

"Be back soon," I promised on my way out the door. My mom was watching the light fade over the mountains. I'm not sure she even heard me.

I hurried to the woods behind the school. It was four o'clock, and I only had about half an hour before dark. I reached the tree fort in less than fifteen minutes. The rope, of course, was pulled up. This was the first time I had come to the fort without Russell or Simon. It was the first time I would have to climb the tree myself.

I found a fallen branch big enough to hold me and leaned it against the trunk of the tree fort. That gave me a leg up, but I could just barely reach the lowest branch. I took off my mittens to get a better grip. I pulled with both my arms and scrambled up to the first branch. From there, the climbing was tricky but not hard. In a minute I had pulled myself into the tree fort.

It was empty. The radio was gone. The blankets were gone. There wasn't so much as a nut or bolt left on the floor.

I sat there, listening to the quiet sounds of the woods. The rustling of a grouse looking for its evening meal. The sighing of the branches as they moved in a silent breeze.

Despite the falling darkness, the truth was plain to see. I was out. Completely out.

23

Coming Clean

I walked out of the woods, following my tracks as the evening light faded to black. I felt a terrible stabbing pain in my chest, as if I had been running miles on a cold winter day. My eyes were hot and dry. I had to blink and blink to stop the stinging.

Simon had lied to me, and the worst part about it was that I couldn't even get mad at him. I tried. I really tried to hate him. I called him all kinds of names in my head: Stinker and Liar and Rat-Breath and Dirty-Low-Down-Cheating-Crumb. But even in that cloud of fury, I could still see Simon's face. I could see the black hair that always fell forward into his eyes, and his thick round glasses, a little bit crooked, and his eyebrows all bunched up from concentrating so hard. And behind Simon, behind him I saw the shadow of Alice, who in my mind looked a lot like me.

I just couldn't hate him. And I desperately wanted to, because that would have made the next part so easy.

I knew as I walked away from the abandoned tree fort that I wasn't going home. I just didn't know exactly where I *was* headed.

My first thought was to go to the Security Office. I had

a pretty good idea where that was located, even though buildings on the Hill had a habit of moving every few months. But something inside told me to stay away from Security.

Nobody on the Hill trusted Security. They were sort of the on-the-premises enemy. I guess it had to be that way. I mean, Security was sent to the Hill to restrict the scientists. And scientists just don't like restrictions. So now that I had to do what I had to do, I didn't really like the idea of doing it with Security, if you know what I mean.

Then the idea of Sergeant McElway popped into my head. He was someone I liked. He was someone I trusted. The only problem was, I didn't know where to find him. I didn't know if he was on duty at the moment, and I certainly couldn't go looking for him in the soldiers' barracks. None of the kids dared go there. I'm not sure I can say exactly why, but it was understood that us kids were not to go anywhere near the soldiers' barracks.

Besides, the more I thought about it, the more I realized that what I had to tell was bigger than a sergeant in the MPs. I needed to find someone in the army who was important, really important. As important as the General himself. The problem was, the General didn't live on the Hill. He lived in Washington, D.C. And I had a better chance of getting in touch with the man in the moon.

In the end, I pointed my feet in the direction of Bathtub Row. That's where the really important people on the Hill lived, in those beautiful old houses that used to be part of the boys' school before the war. And I happened to know that one of the houses on the very northern end of Bathtub Row was the home of a captain in the army.

It was Mrs. Parsons who answered my trembling knock on the door. She didn't seem the least bit surprised to see me. Maybe she thought I was a new friend of her daughter, Peggy. She just whisked me inside and sat me on the couch right in front of the fire. I was shaking, but it wasn't because of the cold March air.

"Ma'am," I said. "Ma'am." I couldn't stop trembling.

"You're Anna's and Paul's little girl, aren't you, dear?" She sat down next to me.

"Yes, Ma'am. Yes. I'm Hazel." I folded my arms tightly across my chest, trying to stop the shakes. But that just seemed to make it worse. I must have looked like some crazy jack-in-the-box, just sprung.

"Have you been outside long, dear? You seem to have the chills." I could see concern creeping over her face. She reached a hand out to feel my forehead. "You're ice, through and through."

"Not too long," I said. The thought kept whirling through my head, *Even now. Even now I can back down. It's not too late to change my mind.* All these pictures kept crowding my brain. I saw Simon with his headphones on. And FDR in front of the White House. And the little boy from Hamburg carrying those two sacks across the Danish border. *How heavy those sacks must have been,* I thought. *How did he manage to carry them so far?* I saw my dad working in his lab. And I saw my mom planting flowers in her garden back home. *Who am I helping and who am I hurting?* I tried to see the faces of all the American soldiers fighting overseas. But I couldn't. I just couldn't see them. There were too many. And I didn't love any of them.

"Well?" asked Mrs. Parsons, as politely as she could.

I realized that I had been sitting there, silent and shaking, for minutes. She was awfully nice, Mrs. Parsons.

"I need to talk to Captain Parsons," I blurted out.

"He's not home, yet, dear. Is there something I can help you with? Is there a problem at home? Is your mother all right?"

She took my hand. She looked really worried now. But just at that moment, the front door opened, and in walked Captain Parsons.

As soon as I saw him, I knew I had made the right choice. The captain was tall, a little older than my dad, and he wore a jacket with stars and bars across the front. On his head was an officer's hat with gold braid. There was no mistaking it: He was important. But he also had bright, happy eyes and a smiling mouth that made it clear he was glad to be home.

Mrs. Parsons stood up immediately. "Deke," she said. "This is Hazel Moore, Paul's little girl. She's come to talk to you about something." She gave her husband a quick peck on the cheek, and in that instant, managed to whisper a few words to him. His face turned serious. Mrs. Parsons went into the kitchen, and the captain sat down in one of the armchairs facing the couch. He crossed his legs and folded his hands, like this kind of thing happened every night.

"What can I do for you?" he asked.

"I've come to see you, Sir, because you're a very important person on the Hill and you're in the army—"

"The navy," he said. "Excuse my interruption, but I'm a captain in the navy, not the army."

That stopped me dead in my tracks. I couldn't think what to do. It was the army that ran the Hill. It was the army that made all the rules and made sure we followed them. The army was the commanding force in our lives. Should I give any of this information to the navy?

"Don't worry, Hazel," said the captain. "You can still talk to me. Technically speaking, the army and the navy are on the same side." His eyes had that twinkle again. Was he taking me seriously?

"I'm here because I think there's a spy on the Hill," I said, surprised at how strong my voice sounded. "I was listening on a short-wave radio, and I heard a voice talking in Russian. The signal was very clear. It had to be coming from the Hill."

The Captain stiffened in his chair. "What short-wave radio?"

"A radio that some of the kids on the Hill built. We've been sending and receiving signals. I know that's not allowed, and I'm very, very sorry. We didn't mean to do anything wrong. We were just having fun." My voice cracked on the last word.

"Who built the radio?"

"I'm not going to tell you that. It's not important to the information about the spy, and I just won't tell you. You or anybody. Sir."

"You're going to have to tell us eventually, Hazel. We need to know."

"No, Sir. I'm sorry. I know I've caused a lot of trouble already, but I'm not going to tell you the names of the other kids. Not ever."

Captain Parsons leaned back in his chair and looked at me long and hard. He looked at the fire and then again at me. Finally, he broke the silence. "Your father is one of the most hardworking men I've ever met." There was another long silence after that. I didn't dare move.

"Well," said the captain after a long while. "I guess the next thing we need to do is call up the boys from Security and let them hear your story."

"Oh, *please*, could we not do that?" I begged. Sitting in this warm living room with this nice man and the comfortable sounds of dinner cooking in the next room was all I could bear. Being brave and strong in front of strangers in a detention cell somewhere on the Hill seemed impossible. "I don't want to talk to Security. I'm afraid of them. I don't know what they'll do to me!"

"I'm afraid Security takes this sort of information very seriously. They're going to have to talk to you."

"Why can't I tell you everything and then you pass it all along to them? Please. I want to do the right thing. I really do. But I don't want to get my friends in trouble, and I don't want to go to jail."

Captain Parson's voice was stern. "First of all, *you* didn't get your friends in trouble. They did that all by themselves when they built a radio that they knew was illegal. I'm guessing that your friends are boys and I'm guessing that they're older than you are. And I'm guessing that they should have known better than to mess with the United States Army."

He paused, and then his tone softened a little. "But I understand your position. And I understand your reluctance to talk to Security. They can be a little rough around the edges. But they have a job to do, and we have to help them do it. So here's what we're going to do."

In the end, he sent for one of the muck-a-mucks from Security and a secretary who took shorthand, and they took my statement right there in Captain Parson's living room. I had to swear on a Bible that I was telling the truth and sign a document a few days later. But I never did give them the names of Simon or Russell, which seemed terribly important to me at the time.

Little did I realize how much the Security men already knew. I would find out the next day.

24

Just a Kid

I walked home, exhausted and alone. Captain Parsons had offered to walk me home, but I said that I would rather go by myself. I think he understood why.

When I got back to our apartment, my mom was right where I'd left her, staring at the black mountains. She'd been doing that a lot lately. It made me nervous, the way she would stare out that window for hours and hours, not even knowing what was going on in the room where she was sitting. But it made my life easier. At least I didn't have to explain to her where I'd been.

I went to bed early that night and slept like the dead. The next morning was Sunday. By the time I got up, Eleanor and her parents were at church. My dad had left for the Tech Area—or maybe he hadn't come home last night—and my mom had taken up her station on the couch.

I poured myself a bowl of cereal and sat down at the kitchen table. On my right arm, just above the elbow, I noticed a small green bruise. A thumbprint.

"There's a square dance tonight," I said. "In Theater No. 2."

"A square dance?" said my mom. It was as if I had just

told her there was going to be a greased pig contest.

"Yeah. A square dance. Swing your partner. Doe-see-doe. It's something people do."

My mother shook her head in disbelief. "Square dancing."

"I guess you're not planning to go."

"Honestly, Hazel. This place doesn't make me feel like dancing."

"Are you feeling sick?" I asked.

"I don't think so," she answered.

"You should go see Dr. Coles," I said. "If you're sick, you need to go to the doctor." It was like a bird that had been circling my head for months had finally landed. The realization, sudden and complete, stunned me—my mom was sick. She needed help.

I stood up from the table and pulled on my coat, mumbling that I was going to see if Eleanor was back yet. I ran to the Tech Area and told the guard that I needed to see my father, right away. It was a matter of life and death. He came out a minute later, his coat over his arm, prepared for the worst.

"What's happened?" he asked.

I pulled him away from the guardhouse. "Dad. We need to do something. About Mom. She isn't doing so great."

My father looked at me. Oh, he looked old! As if he had lived three lifetimes in our year on the Hill.

"No," he answered, putting his arm around my shoulder. We started to walk around Ashley Pond. "She isn't doing so great. But she's going to be fine, once the war is over. She'll be right as rain when we all go home."

"We can't wait until then," I said. "She should go see Dr. Coles right away."

"It's not that simple, Hazel. Dr. Coles is a good doctor. But he doesn't have the cure for what ails your mom."

"What is it? What's making her sick?" I had a need, like a deep thirst, to believe that my dad had all the answers.

"Your mom, you see, doesn't belong here," he said. "This isn't the right place for a woman like her."

"You mean she's not like the other mothers?"

"It's more than that," he said. "Much more. Your mom has very high ideals, very fine sensibilities, deep beliefs. She's offended by, oh, by a lot of things. Hypocrisy, dishonesty, self-aggrandizement. Do you know what all those words mean?"

"I don't know what self-aggrandizement is."

"It's when you think you're the most important person in the world. When you forget that there are other people living their lives, and those lives are just as important as yours." My dad stood silently for a minute. He looked across the still water of the pond. "I guess that's my crime. Self-aggrandizement. Working night and day, spending all my time thinking about my work, I guess I forgot that I wasn't the center of the universe. Your mom tried to remind me. But then I guess she gave up."

"Maybe you should tell her that you remember now. Maybe it would make her feel better."

"I think it's a little too late for that. But don't worry, Hazel. As soon as we get home, back to Montclair, she'll come around. She just needs a change of scenery. She just needs to get off the Hill. This war can't last forever."

I needed to believe him. It was all I had.

We had circled the pond once. My dad stopped walking in front of the Tech Area guardhouse.

"Dad?" I said. "There's a square dance tonight."

"Well, have a good time, honey," he said. "I'll be thinking of you." But I knew he wouldn't. Not his fault, he just wouldn't.

The square dance was like something out of a movie, except all the actors in costume were people I knew. The moms wore prairie skirts and peasant blouses. The men wore jeans and flannel shirts with bolo ties looped around their necks. The GI band that usually played brassy dance tunes on Saturday nights was hammering out a country two-step on two fiddles and a bass.

Even Eleanor wore a costume. She had on a blue-and-white gingham dress with a starched white apron, which reminded me of Dorothy in *The Wizard of Oz*. Her black hair was braided and looped around her head. Only her cowboy boots were familiar. She kept pulling me onto the dance floor at the start of every new song, and I kept pulling her off the dance floor at the end of every song. It was more like a tug-of-war than dancing.

Eleanor was the first to notice. She's got antennae when it comes to gossip. She nudged me and pointed across the dance floor. "What's up?" she asked.

A few of the grownups had their heads bent together, whispering. One woman broke away and whispered something to the woman next to her. A girl we knew from Central School ran across the room and started talking furiously with some friends.

"Come on," said Eleanor, walking off the floor in the middle of a song. Eleanor walked right up to the girl and asked, "What's up?"

She hardly needed to ask. The girl was spilling her story to anyone within shouting distance. "They've arrested two boys for having a radio. They've been sending signals. Probably to the enemy! One of them might be German. He has a funny name. The MPs have them in custody and they're probably going to be tried for treason!"

"Who?" asked Eleanor. "Who?"

"No one knows, except the MPs," said the girl. "They've got them in seclusion!"

"I need to sit down," I said, pulling on Eleanor's arm.

"You don't look so good," she said, pushing me over to a folding chair on the side of the room. "Are you going to throw up?"

"I don't think so. This room is hot. I feel like I can't breathe."

Eleanor fanned me for a minute with an empty plate. "I'll get my mom," she said.

"No! I feel fine now. I'm going home."

"I'll walk you," said Eleanor.

"Don't. You'd just have to walk back. It would be a waste of time. I'll be fine."

"Can you believe it about those boys?" said Eleanor. "What kind of crumb would do that? Rat out his own country during a war? I wish I knew who they were."

One more secret. The last, I vowed.

Once outside, I headed straight for Simon's house. The night air was cold, but I was in such a hurry that I didn't even bother to button up my coat as I ran to McKeeville.

The lights were on in Simon's living room, but the shades were drawn. I checked each window until I found one where the shade wasn't pulled all the way down. Peeking through the one-inch crack, I could see Simon's mom and dad in the living room. They were having a tremendous argument, but their voices were low enough that I couldn't make out any of the words. They were both dressed for the square dance, as if they'd been getting ready when they got the news.

I sneaked around to the back. I tapped on Simon's window. Within seconds, the window slid open a crack.

"Hey," I said, putting my mouth to the crack. "How's it going?" Just as if we had run into each other at the PX.

"Okay, I guess."

With the window open, I could hear his parents' voices crashing against the thin walls of Simon's bedroom. We both looked toward the closed door, as if the angry words might batter it to the ground.

"They're really having it out, huh?" I said.

"Yeah. They don't get along so great in the best of times. When something like this happens, they really come apart. You should have heard them the whole time my sister was sick. They were at each other's throats."

"So I guess the MPs found the radio?"

"Yeah. They tracked us the last time we moved it. I guess they were closer than I thought. They asked me about the spy right away, but I didn't really have any more information than you'd already given them."

"I didn't give them your name, you know. I wouldn't do it, no matter how many times they asked."

"Yeah, I know."

"Did they . . . did they torture you?" I asked.

"You're such a numbskull, Hazel. I swear. You don't even have the brains to come in out of the cold." Simon opened the window all the way and hoisted me in. I landed headfirst on the floor. Without bothering to help me up, Simon flopped on the bed where he'd been reading a book, a trashy detective paperback called *The Man from Beyond Midnight*. I sat down at the other end, kicked off my shoes, and tucked my feet under the blanket.

"So what d'ya think?" I asked. "Do you think it was really a Russian spy we heard? What did the Security guys say?"

"Security guys don't give *out* information," said Simon. "But they seemed pretty interested in the story. They asked me to repeat every detail about a hundred times. And," he couldn't keep the pride out of his voice, "they were *really* impressed with my radio."

Simon stared at the ceiling. His long legs dangled over the edge of the bed.

"I'm sorry that you lost your radio, Simon."

"Hey. There's a war going on. We all need to make sacrifices, right?"

"I never wanted to rat on you, you know. I just thought it was the right thing to do. Deep inside, I thought it was right."

"Yeah, I know. The thing is, Hazel, it *was* the right thing to do. And I knew it too. I just didn't have the guts to do it. But you've always had more guts than me, more than me and Russell put together. That was obvious the first day we met."

Me? Guts? I liked that idea. It was new.

"So, Simon. What are they going to do to you? Are you going to jail?" My heart broke at the thought of Simon locked in a cell.

Simon laughed. "That's the funny thing. They're not going to do anything. They figure I'm just a kid. What does a kid matter?" He sounded offended. I think it hurt his feelings to have the army treat him like a child. Boys! They always think they're so much more grownup than they are!

"But my parents!" he said. "That's another story. They're trying to decide right now whether I should be grounded until I'm eighteen or sent away to a private boarding school for delinquent minors. They think I'm going to land in jail one day. What yo-yos. They don't get it at all. They think life on the Hill is just grand."

"If you want, Simon, I'll speak in your defense." I *thought* that was the proper term, but it made Simon laugh.

"Nah. That's okay. But thanks for the offer."

We sat without saying anything for a minute.

"You better be going home," he said. "I'll help you out." He boosted me over the windowsill, just like he used to boost me up the trunk of the tree to reach the lowest knot on the rope.

I could still hear Simon's parents arguing as I walked away. Until I heard the rattle and thump of Simon closing his window. Then everything was quiet.

25

In Pain

It seemed to happen overnight. But of course, it couldn't have really come on that quickly. And in fact, once we thought about it, none of us had seen Dinah for at least two days before we found her lying in a corner of the furnace room.

It was the end of March and still winter cold. Simon had been shipped off to live with a very strict aunt and uncle in Vermont.

"Better than a reform school," he grumbled as he got on the bus. "But not by much."

A raw wind blew across the mesa as I waved goodbye. When the bus disappeared from sight, I looked at the canyon beyond. Not a single flower bloomed in the hillsides, not a leaf could be found on even one aspen tree.

So it wasn't surprising that Dinah looked for a warm spot to die.

Except she wasn't dead. That was the horrible part.

Mr. Gonzales found her first. He was the old Spanish handyman who tended the furnace in our house. All winter long, he slept in the room below our apartment and shoveled coal into the great roaring hold of the furnace. Our apartments were always too hot, and when we tried to tell this to Mr. Gonzales, he seemed very proud, as if we were congratulating him on a job well done.

Eleanor and I were playing Parcheesi in her living room when we heard a metal tapping on the front door. It was Mr. Gonzales wearing his usual outfit, overalls and a fedora, and carrying his trusty short-handled shovel.

"*Señorita*," he said. "*El gato*. . ."

He led us, without another word, to the sooty confines of the furnace room. The minute we walked into the tiny room we noticed the stink. It was like being hit over the head with a hammer. One time in Montclair, I found a squirrel that had been dead in our attic for a few days. That's what the room smelled like.

I covered my mouth and nose with my arm and turned to run out the door, but Eleanor didn't turn back. With his shovel, Mr. Gonzales pointed to the far corner of the room. Eleanor followed where he pointed. I came halfway into the room, still covering my nose and trying not to faint.

Dinah lay stretched out, her paws in front of her, her head lolling back. She had thrown up recently, and a small puddle of vomit lay on the floor in front of her mouth. Something was wrong, very wrong. A huge lump swelled under the skin along her lower jaw. Where the lump was, there was no fur, and thick yellow stuff oozed out of the bare skin. She reeked like something dead dragged out of a swamp.

"Go get my mother," said Eleanor as she pulled off her sweater and wrapped it around Dinah. Dinah seemed to flinch when Eleanor touched her, but she didn't make a sound.

I ran to the Tech Area gate. The MPs blocked my way. "You have to get Mrs. Talbot," I shrieked. "It's an emergency."

The MPs didn't even move. Nothing ruffled them.

"What's the emergency?" one of them drawled.

I didn't even think before saying, "It's her daughter. She's very sick. She might be dying!"

Both MPs straightened up. They bent their heads together in a brief conference. "Regulations require a written summons before calling someone out of Gamma Building." The older MP looked at me closely. He shifted his weight from one leg to the other and scratched slowly underneath his collar. "Aw, hell. Since it's her daughter." He nodded to the other MP, who disappeared. Less than three minutes later Mrs. Talbot came tearing through the gate. She was frantically trying to pull on her coat, but one of the sleeves was inside out. She made desperate stabbing motions with her arm, all the time running as fast as she could in her high-heel shoes.

"Where is she, Hazel? For God's sake. Did she fall? Does she have a fever?"

When we turned the corner and were out of sight of the MPs, I came clean. "It's not Eleanor who's sick. It's Dinah."

Mrs. Talbot stopped dead in her tracks and gave me such a look, I thought she was going to slap me. I took a step back.

"You girls!" She sounded really mad. "You girls have got to stop playing these tricks. Torturing the MPs, sneaking out the window at all hours, and now this. Listen to me, Miss. You may think this is just some funny joke. That what we're doing on the Hill is just some sort of lark for your everlasting amusement. And that pulling me out of work to baby sit a cat with the sniffles is fine and dandy! But let me tell you . . ." She raised her hand and I really thought she was going to hit me, she was that angry. I'd never been hit in all my life, and I didn't know what to do.

"But, Mrs. Talbot," I blurted out. "It isn't the sniffles! It's horrible, you can't imagine. Her whole face! She looks like a monster! And I really do think she's dying!"

Mrs. Talbot dropped her hand. "Oh honestly," she said. "It's only a cat." But she sounded more like the Mrs. Talbot I knew. We hurried off, without another word, to the furnace room.

When we got there, the room was empty.

"She must have taken Dinah to the hospital," I said.

In less than five minutes, we were walking into the hospital lobby. The receptionist took us straight into the examination room.

Dr. Coles was bent over the motionless body of the cat. It was shocking how small Dinah looked lying on the table. Eleanor stood over to the side, her arms folded tightly across her chest.

When Mrs. Talbot saw Dinah's face, she gasped, and her hand flew to her mouth. Dr. Coles never even looked

174

up. He continued his examination, delicately probing the cat's jaw with a tongue depressor. When at last he finished, he led Mrs. Talbot to a far corner of the room and spoke in a voice just above a whisper.

"It's a necrosis of the jaw bone. Clearly the result of contact with a reactive material. Perhaps something she came across behind the Tech Area. Your security clearance gives you some idea of the nature of the materials found there. The level of the radioactive poisoning is high enough to ensure that the animal will not recover."

"Oh, dear. Oh, dear," whispered Mrs. Talbot, slowly shaking her head. She made a quiet clicking sound with her tongue, and then she took a deep breath. "Then the kindest thing is simply to end the poor cat's suffering." Mrs. Talbot turned to face Eleanor, but Dr. Coles laid a hand on her elbow, pulling her back into conference with him. He whispered in her ear, and Mrs. Talbot nodded her head. The only word I could make out was "research."

"Whatever you think is best," said Mrs. Talbot. She had already given up on Dinah. She had bigger worries on her mind. She put her arms around Eleanor and said, "It's time for us to go home."

"Not without Dinah," said Eleanor.

"Dinah's not coming home with us, dear. Not today. Not ever. She's very sick. She's in pain. Dr. Coles is going to end her misery."

"Not without Dinah."

Mrs. Talbot tried quiet reasoning and then gentle threats. But whenever she or Dr. Coles laid a hand on her, Eleanor started to bite and scratch. I squeezed myself into a corner of the room. This was family business. In the end, two nurses held Eleanor down while Dr. Coles gave her a shot to calm her. It was just awful.

That evening, I stopped upstairs to see how Eleanor was doing. Mrs. Talbot answered the door looking worn out. I think she'd been crying, but you can never tell with grownups.

"She doesn't want to see anyone, dear," explained Mrs. Talbot. "But come by tomorrow. I'm sure she'll be just fine by tomorrow."

Grownups are so dumb sometimes.

26

Tears, Finally

Every day for the next three weeks, Eleanor went to the hospital and asked to see Dinah. Every day, she was told by Dr. Coles that Dinah had been put to sleep. That Dinah was in heaven. That Dinah was at peace.

But Eleanor wasn't. She refused to go to school. She wouldn't leave her room. And she wouldn't see anybody. Not even me.

In the middle of all this, I turned thirteen. My first birthday on the Hill. Not that anybody noticed. Who was left to care?

The day after my birthday, I decided enough was enough. Eleanor was my best friend, and she was just going to have to get over losing her cat. After all, she still had me. Wasn't that enough?

After lunch, I climbed the stairs to Eleanor's apartment and marched right into her room. I had kind of expected the door to be closed and locked and maybe even barricaded with her dresser or something. But her door was wide open. She lay on top of her neatly made bed, all dressed and with her hair combed and pulled back with a barrette.

"Eleanor!" I said. "Get out of bed!"

She looked at me. Then she turned and looked out the window.

"Oh, come on, Eleanor," I pleaded. "This is too much. Really. You can't stay in your room forever. Everybody at school misses you. Mrs. Wilson misses you. And Mrs. Inglis, too. All the girls miss you, and even some of the boys." What I wanted to say was, "I miss you." But the words stuck in my throat.

Eleanor didn't say anything. She didn't look sad. Or angry. Or anything. She just stared out the window.

Now I was scared. This wasn't the Eleanor I knew. This was like a robot of Eleanor. Or a shadow. Or an old faded photograph.

"Look, Eleanor. I'm sorry Dinah's dead. We're all . . ."

"Dinah's not dead." Eleanor said this the way she might have said she had had eggs for breakfast. Not a good thing. Not a bad thing. Just a fact.

"Eleanor. She really is. She got sick. Remember? We found her in the furnace room and we took her to Dr. Coles and he put her to sleep."

"Dinah's not dead."

I put my hands on my hips. This was infuriating. I didn't mind Eleanor feeling sad or holing up in her room or deserting me or even forgetting my birthday. But I was not about to let her get away with a complete misrepresentation of the facts. The fact was Dinah was dead. And Eleanor was just going to have to accept that.

"She's dead, Eleanor. Listen to me. She's dead."

I never saw the book coming at me, it was that fast. It

struck me, flat, on the shoulder, and almost knocked me over. I recovered my balance just in time to see Eleanor hurling a glass of water at me. Next came her alarm clock and a box of tissues. Anything she could lay her hands on, she threw at me.

My first instinct was to run out of the room, but for some reason, I just kept dodging, all the time moving in closer to the bed. The closer I got, the more things hit me square on, but the less they hurt. When I was a foot away, I pounced, landing right on top of Eleanor and squashing her flat on the bed.

Of course, it only took her about two seconds to flip me over and pin me. I couldn't move my arms or legs. And I wasn't finding it so easy to breathe. Eleanor weighed at least twenty pounds more than me, and she was pressing down for all she was worth.

She sat on me for about a minute, but it felt like an hour. When she stood up, all she said was, "Come on. Let's go."

She grabbed the pillow off her bed and rummaged in her closet for some rope—the same rope we used when we went adventuring in the canyons. It was long, at least thirty feet, with knots tied in it for easy climbing. She walked out the front door, and I followed.

We walked the three minutes to the hospital in complete silence. I expected her to go in the front door, but instead she walked around to the back. One of the windows was open a crack. There were a bunch of empty wooden crates tossed there, but most of them were too flimsy to stand on. Eleanor finally found one that seemed a little more sturdy than the rest. She stood it on end beneath the open window, then climbed on top. She could reach the open window, but she wasn't tall enough to pull herself inside.

"Give me a boost up," I said. "I can get in."

I climbed onto the crate. It groaned, like it was about to break into a million pieces. Eleanor made a cradle with her hands and boosted me up. I was just able to push up the window, stick my head in, and wriggle through.

I sort of dangled inside, then fell to the floor like a sack of potatoes. For a moment, I lay perfectly still, my heart pounding. I expected a nurse or even Dr. Coles to come charging into the room. But nobody came.

I jumped to my feet and looked around. I was in one of the exam rooms. Luckily, there was a small cart on wheels. I pushed it under the window and climbed on top of it. I poked my head out just long enough for Eleanor to toss me the rope. Then I climbed down and tied the rope to the leg of the heavy metal desk on the opposite end of the room. I tied three good knots, then one more just to be safe. I tugged on the rope three times—our signal for all systems go.

In less than a minute, Eleanor had climbed up the rope and through the window. She tossed the pillow into the room, then jumped down, landing on her feet without making a sound.

Just like spies, we worked our way through the hospital, peeking into each room as we went. It was lunchtime on a slow day, and the halls were completely empty. Finally, we came to a doorway with a frosted glass window pane marked Lab A.

The door was unlocked. We crept in. The room was large and airy and smelled a little bit of floor wax and antiseptic. There was one long black lab table in the middle of the room. Along the walls were several cluttered desks and bookshelves filled with rows of reference books. A cupboard with glass doors held flasks, burners, pipettes, and black rubber tubing.

I was the one who discovered the crate on top of the desk at the far end of the room. One side of the crate was cut away so that the box was open on its top and front. A blanket was carefully draped over the crate to block out the sun. I lifted the blanket, afraid of what I would see.

Inside, Dinah lay on a cushion, unmoving. Her wound was clean and dressed. But her tongue was swollen to the size of my hand and hung out of her mouth like some dead animal. Her fur had fallen out in patches all over her body so that she was more bald than covered. Her glazed eyes were half open, but unseeing, and she breathed with the greatest difficulty, as if every breath were a misery.

My first thought was to get Eleanor out of there as fast as I could. I would lie. I would say I felt sick. I would say I was going to throw up. I would call for a nurse if I had to. Anything to get her out of the hospital before she saw Dinah.

But even as I was figuring out a plan, Eleanor came up

behind me. I tried to drop the blanket, but it was too late. She leaned into the crate crooning, "There's my little girl. There's my Dinah puss."

I moved aside. Eleanor lay her head next to Dinah's and slowly stroked her few remaining patches of fur, all the while cooing and whispering to her. Dinah never lifted her head, but I think she knew that Eleanor was there.

And then Eleanor sang a lullaby to her.

> *Irene, goodnight,*
> *Irene, goodnight,*
> *Goodnight Irene, goodnight Irene,*
> *I'll kiss you in my dreams.*

So gently, so sweetly, and all the while singing the lullaby, Eleanor put the pillow over Dinah and held it there, for minute after minute, and then finally lay her own head on top and closed her eyes.

The room was as silent as a tomb. I strained to catch the sound of another human voice, any voice, but all I could hear was the rushing of blood in my ears. It was as if the whole world had died and passed into the next world. What would we do now? I didn't know.

But Eleanor did.

Carefully, she lifted Dinah and arranged her on the pillow. Holding both in her arms—like a servant presenting a gift to a king—she walked out of the lab, down the hallway, past the receptionist, and out of the hospital. I walked behind, her silent attendant.

We walked down the main street, past the fancy houses

on Bathtub Row, and straight into Fuller Lodge.

I had been looking for the comfort of human voices, and here they were. Table after table was filled with grownups, chatting and laughing, talking and gossiping. Some were serious, some were merry. Some seemed in a hurry; others were lingering over steaming cups of coffee. But they all had one thing in common. Not one of them expected to see a girl carrying a dead cat walk into Fuller Lodge that day.

As we passed each table, the people seated there fell silent. It was like watching dominoes fall, one by one, as table after table was silenced. Finally we reached the far end of Fuller Lodge, and the entire dining room was as quiet as a graveyard. Dr. Coles always ate lunch at the corner table at the end of Fuller Lodge. He was there that day, sitting with his wife and some men in uniform. At his place were the leftovers of his meal: the bones of a chicken breast and a few scattered green beans. A half-eaten brownie, swimming in a puddle of vanilla ice cream, sat next to his coffee cup, which had just been filled.

Eleanor stopped in front of Dr. Coles. She held out Dinah as if she were presenting a crown at some important ceremony. No one in the room moved. No one breathed. Everyone watched Eleanor and the doctor to see what would happen next.

"You are a terrible man," said Eleanor in a voice that was strong with the truth of her words. "A terrible, terrible man. Shame on you. Shame. Look at what you've done. Look at it!"

She held up the evidence of his crime for everyone to see. Doctor Coles didn't move. No one moved. Eleanor's words seemed to hold them all in a spell.

"You call this science?" she said. "This isn't science. It's death."

And then she marched out of Fuller Lodge. But I couldn't follow. I had no business going where Eleanor had to go, doing what she had to do.

Instead, I was left staring at Dr. Coles, and he at me. I looked at his face, and I tried to *hate* him. Tried to hate him for what he had done to Dinah on purpose and what he had done to Eleanor by mistake. I wanted to see the evil villain that Eleanor did. I felt like I owed her that, at the very least.

But I couldn't. I saw a face, just a face, with a look of sorrow in its eyes and a few crumbs on its chin. I was reminded of my dad. My dad was a scientist, too, like Dr. Coles. I could hear his calm voice. I could hear him say how important research is. I knew that Dr. Coles had made Dinah suffer so that he could learn something important—what happens to the body when it's exposed to radiation. I knew that this information would be terribly important if someday a person was poisoned by radiation. "Knowledge is power," my dad often said. And I knew what he would say if he were Dr. Coles: The suffering of one cat is a small price to pay for knowledge.

I couldn't hate Dr. Coles. I couldn't hate my dad. Not even for Eleanor.

After Eleanor walked out, all eyes turned to me. And

still, no one moved. No one spoke. It was like we were all frozen in a moment, caught under a spell, and none of us knew how to break it.

And that's when I broke down and cried. Rivers of tears, mountains of pain. Sobbing in a way I hadn't cried since I was a baby.

I cried for Eleanor, and I cried for Dinah. I cried for Mrs. Sanchez who had lost a son, and Severo who had lost his life. I cried for my father who had lost his wife, and my mother who had lost her spirit.

But mostly I cried for myself. Because I was an orphan. And deep in my heart, I knew that everything would *not* be all right, even after we got home to Montclair. My family was broken into pieces, like a china doll dropped on a stone floor. And nothing would ever be the same again.

27

From Bad to Worse

Less than a month after Dinah died, Eleanor and her mom moved back to Chicago. It all happened so fast. On Friday, Eleanor told me that they were leaving, and by Tuesday, they were boarding the bus to Lamy. At the Lamy depot, they would catch the Santa Fe Chief, which would take them all the way back to Chicago.

"It's all for the best, dear," said Mrs. Talbot as I helped her and Eleanor pack boxes of clothes to be shipped by train. "This is just no place for children," she said, and then added in a hurry, "Of course, you'll be fine."

Eleanor and I spent one more day hiking in the canyons. We painted our toenails *Victory Red* one last time, and went to our final Saturday matinee double feature. Then we had to say good-bye.

We had already made plans for when I would visit Chicago and how she would come to Montclair and we would go see the Rockettes at Radio City Music Hall. But it didn't make the good-bye any easier.

The same rag-tag army bus that had brought me up the Hill a year ago was now ready to take Eleanor away from me. At the last possible minute, Eleanor hugged me close and then squeezed my hand and jumped on the bus.

As it pulled away, I looked in my hand and found a crumpled up ball of paper. I opened it up, and it said, "You are TGTBT. Best friends. Always."

I waved and waved and waved at the bus until it dropped off the mesa.

And then on Thursday, the news broke. It spread like wildfire across the Hill. From my window, I saw several people run from house to house, knocking on doors as if the whole town was on fire. Since none of us had telephones, this was the only way important news could travel. I ran out onto the porch and called to one of the people in the street. "What's going on? What happened?"

The man who stopped was a carpenter, a big Texan who had won a contest last spring for splitting the most wood in five minutes. Tears streamed down his face. "Roosevelt is dead. He was bleeding in his brain, and they couldn't save him! The president is dead."

I went back inside the house. My mom was in her bedroom, looking at photos in an old family album. I sat in the living room and wondered why the sun was still shining. Why the mountains hadn't moved or the earth stopped turning. *What will become of us now?* I wondered. Without Roosevelt, we were lost. Without him, the war would never end.

The whole Hill mourned. That Sunday, Oppie led a memorial service. My dad and I trudged through the snow that had fallen in the night and gathered with the others in Theater No. 2 to hear words that might give comfort. My mom stayed home. All through the service, I found myself wishing desperately that Eleanor was still on the Hill.

Oppie said, "Man is a creature whose substance is faith. What his faith is, he is." He told us to hold on to our faith and to let our faith lead us to hope for a better world. Everybody in the room cried buckets. And I cried a little, too. Lately, I was finding it easier and easier to cry.

Less than a month later, we learned that Hitler was dead. A week after that, Germany surrendered, and the war in Europe was finally over. People all over the Hill poured out of their houses, poured out of the PX and the commissary, even out of the Tech Area and danced and hugged and wept together in the streets. I have never been kissed so many times in my life.

I raced inside to tell my mom the news.

"It's over! It's over! The war in Europe is over!"

She was in bed, awake. But she seemed frightened by my news, instead of happy.

"How did it end?" she asked.

"It just did. The Germans surrendered, and now it's over."

"Not with a bang, but with a whimper," she murmured.

"Aren't you happy?" I asked.

"Of course. The end of war is always a good thing." But she didn't look happy. She looked the way she always did these days. Distracted and sad.

The next day I got up early to see my dad before he went to work. I caught him just as he was heading out the door.

"Are we going home?" I asked. "Now that the war is over?"

He was worn out. His day hadn't even begun, and he looked like he could sleep for a week. "Not just yet. There's still the war in Japan. For some reason, the Japanese don't like the sound of unconditional surrender. They seem hell-bent on dying to the last man."

If I thought winning the war in Europe would make life on the Hill more bearable, I couldn't have been more wrong. If anything, it got worse.

---- **28** ----

Help

It was after Roosevelt's death that my mom completely stopped leaving the house. She had been going out less and less—once a week to the commissary to buy groceries and once a week to the laundry to wash our clothes. But after his death, she stopped completely. She did our laundry in the bathtub. And I started making the weekly trip to the PX myself.

It's funny, because the less she went out, the more I found myself staying in too. I just had this feeling, anytime I was out, that I might be needed at home.

So I got into a new routine. After school, I went straight home. Sometimes my mom would be asleep, sometimes awake. She kept odd hours these days. She was awake a lot at night, and she slept in late in the mornings. Most afternoons she was up when I got home, but she would take catnaps throughout the day.

There was usually something that needed doing: laundry, grocery shopping, picking up the mail, or housecleaning. That kept me busy all afternoon. And then, almost before I knew it, it was time to make dinner.

Making dinner was tough. I had watched my mom cook a lot of times, but I had never learned to do it properly.

To make matters worse, my mom didn't own a single cookbook. She cooked by intuition.

In the end, I made a lot of tuna salad and meat loaf. And none of us starved.

But one afternoon, I ran into Mrs. Perrotta at the commissary. I was trying to figure out which cans had green beans in them. None of the canned foods at the commissary had labels on them. The cans were all identical and painted that same army-issue green. To figure out what was inside, you had to read the label on the shelf, which was sometimes in the wrong place or just plain missing.

Mrs. Perrotta asked me about school and whether I'd heard from Eleanor lately.

"We miss your mother at our Lecture Committee meetings," she said kindly. "Tell her, please, that I asked about her. Will you, dear?"

I promised to pass along the message, but I knew I wouldn't. My mom didn't like to hear about anything that was happening on the Hill. She didn't want to be reminded of that life out there. I said good-bye to Mrs. Perrotta.

That afternoon, I heard a knock on the door. It had been so long since anyone had stopped by, I almost thought of not answering. But when I opened the door, there was Mrs. Perrotta, holding a large baking dish with a clean towel over the top.

"Oh, Hazel," she said. "I made such a stupid mistake! I thought I was having company over for dinner tonight, so I made two lasagnas. But then I remembered that my company isn't coming until *tomorrow* night. I swear if my head weren't attached to my body, I would lose it at least twice a day. Would you do me a *great* favor and take this extra lasagna off my hands?"

I took the steaming dish and said thanks.

And from then on, at least three times a week, there came a knock on the door and one of the Hill mothers was there with a hot dinner and some cockeyed excuse about why she had too much food at her house. The whole thing became almost funny.

But it was Mrs. Hornridge who saved me at the laundry.

Doing the wash each week was my *least* favorite chore. First of all, the laundry was a five-minute walk from our house. Some weeks I had to make three trips just to get all our dirty clothes there. Second, the wringers for squeezing out the wet clothes were almost impossible to turn, especially if the clothes were sopping wet because the power had gone out during the rinse. And the mangles for ironing the sheets—impossible. I could never get the sheets to go in straight. They came out twice as wrinkled as they went in.

Out of desperation, I had taken to wearing shirts and pants several times between washings and each pair of underwear twice—once outside out and once inside out—to try to cut down on our dirty wash. Even so, I was always behind on laundry.

But one day, early in May, I showed up at the laundry

with an enormous load of wash, and there was Mrs. Hornridge. The laundry was always a busy place, but usually it was the Indian maids who were there. Most of the wives of the scientists didn't do their own wash. Mrs. Hornridge had also just arrived, and she was sorting her clothes into four different baskets. After she asked how my mom and dad were doing, she paused in her sorting as if an idea had just occurred to her.

"Say, Hazel," she said. "Look at this. I bet I don't have enough clothes to do a white wash alone, and I bet you don't either. Why don't I just throw your whites in with mine and we'll do one load together? We can do the same with our darks and brights and delicates."

"I guess," I said. "But it seems like a lot of clothes to do at one time."

"Pish. It'll be done in a jiffy," she said. "I'll use these four machines here. That way, there'll only be one of us paying the army thirty cents an hour instead of two." And she gave me a sly wink, as if we were really pulling one over on the General. "You go on home. I'll bring the washed clothes by your house when they're ready. It's right on my way." And she shooed me out of the laundry.

From then on, one of the moms always happened to stop at our apartment on the way to the laundry at least once a week.

It was pretty obvious what was going on. The moms on the Hill put two and two together, and they did what came naturally to them—they reached out a hand to help. Was I embarrassed by my incompetence? Yes. Was I relieved to have help? You better believe it. Let's face facts: I was thirteen and too young to be running a house on my own.

But mostly, my feelings about all these helpful moms were all tangled up in a big knot of shame. I was ashamed that my own mom was unable to take care of us. And I had never, ever in my whole life been ashamed of my mom. It was a feeling I didn't know what to do with. So I bottled it up and hid it away.

29

Rumors

It was a summer of rumors. One after another swept through the town and choked us with fear. The first came early in June, just two weeks before our scheduled final exams. One of the wives of the scientists got sick with some sort of virus. She was paralyzed from it and then suddenly died. Everyone thought it was polio. There were rumors that it would sweep through the town, that all the children would get it. Central School was closed. All trips to Santa Fe were suspended. Everyone kept their kids inside. No one was allowed to play outside.

Mrs. Perrotta was so worried, she sent Gemma to spend the summer with a friend in California. For the third time in three months, I stood waving as I watched a bus take a friend of mine away from the Hill. I waved for all I was worth. Then I walked back to my apartment. Alone.

The second rumor came in early July. We'd been having a drought since the spring, and the summer was hotter than usual. Houses, rubbish, wood sheds, dry brush—anything that could catch on fire did. Some days, the fire trucks screamed by my house three or four times. It was like the whole town was burning.

Suddenly, folks started saying that the Hill was about

to run out of water completely. That the water pipes were almost dry and soon there wouldn't be enough for drinking, let alone washing dishes or brushing teeth. People started hoarding water in anything that would hold it—bottles, pots, even coffee cups lined up on the kitchen counter like soldiers in a drill.

But it was the third rumor that scared us the most. It was the third one that seemed too fantastic to be true—but what if it was?

I heard it first at the PX. A group of GIs talking, drinking beer and getting a little loud.

"I'm not kidding," said one. "I've been driving them back and forth for weeks now. They're saying the air could catch fire. All of it! It could catch fire and burn, and there'd be no way to put it out."

"What a pile of horse crap," said another. "How can the air burn?"

"You watch," said the first. "You watch how many wives and kids leave the Hill this week. The scientists know. They'll get their families off the Hill. The rest of us can burn in hell, but they'll make sure their families are safe. You watch!"

When the soldiers got to drinking, the PX wasn't a place to be. I paid for my soda and scooted out. But I didn't go home.

I went to the commissary. We were out of milk and eggs. When I walked in, I noticed a knot of mothers over by the meat counter. There was Mrs. Bacher and Mrs. Jette and a few others I didn't know. I pretended to be looking at the meat in the case so I could overhear their talk.

". . . to Michigan on the first train we can get," said Mrs. Bacher. "Robert says it's just not worth taking any chances."

"Does anyone know exactly when the test is going to be?" asked Mrs. Jette. She was talking in a whisper, but I held my breath to hear.

"None of the men will say," answered Mrs. Bacher. "But Robert wants us off the Hill *now*, so it must be soon."

After that, their voices dropped so low, I couldn't catch a word.

And sure enough, a lot of the moms and kids on the Hill disappeared. Just packed up and went off to visit relatives. I noticed. I saw.

The gadget was finally going to be tested! But where? And when?

I started making regular trips to the three places I was most likely to overhear gossip: the PX, the commissary, and the laundry. But my timing must have been off, because I never caught another word about the test. Just the usual gripes about life on the Hill and an occasional bit of scandal. Still, I kept my ears open.

It was a prickly summer. Everyone was on edge. It was like there was electricity in the air. My dad was just about never around. But when he was, he was so jumpy, I couldn't say boo to him without him hitting the roof. I could tell that something was about to happen.

I held my breath and waited.

30

A Circle on the Map

I didn't have to wait long. It was early evening, just a few days after I had first heard the rumor in the PX. I was washing up the dinner dishes. My mom was in her bedroom. The front door opened, and in walked my dad. I was so surprised, I dropped the dish I was holding. Luckily, it didn't break, but it fell right on my bare foot and nearly broke my toe.

"Hazel," he said. "I need to tell you something."

He sat on the couch and motioned for me to sit next to him. I grabbed hold of my foot and hopped over to the couch.

"I want to talk to you before I tell your mother." He seemed very agitated and very tired at the same time. "We're coming to the end of this. At least I hope it's the end. But I need to go away for a few days. I can't tell you where or why. I'm not even supposed to tell you for how long. But I expect I'll be back in three days. Or maybe four. It won't be more than four. Can you manage without me?"

"Yes," I said. "I think so." But deep down, I did *not* think so. My toe was throbbing, and now my head started to ache. I had lost one parent. Was I losing the other? *Would* he be back in four days? He didn't sound sure. I felt as though I'd been living in a box for months, and now the lid of the box was closing shut.

"What about Mom?" I asked. "She won't like it that you're gone."

My father breathed out a long, thin stream of air. "I know. You'll have to help her through. Promise me you'll take care of her. Okay?"

What kind of grownup asks a kid to do that? I gulped. "I promise."

"I need to get a few things together. And I need to talk to your mother. Then I'm off."

"Tonight? You're leaving tonight?" I felt a panic rising in my throat.

"We have to travel at night. It's a six-hour trip, and it's too hot during the day." He went into the bedroom. I heard my father's voice through the thin walls, but I didn't hear my mom answer. In a minute he came out with one clean shirt and a pair of underwear. He put the clothes in a paper sack, and then prepared a Thermos full of black coffee and three large liverwurst sandwiches.

"Okay," he said. "I'm going. This is really the end, Hazel. I promise. After this, we can all go home and . . . and everything will be fine. Better than ever."

He kissed me once on the top of my head, and then walked out.

After he left, I walked down the hall and was surprised to find my mother standing in the doorway.

"Did he tell you where he was going?" she asked.

I shook my head. "It's top secret."

"Top secret. The top secret. The secret of all secrets. Let's listen for trucks leaving from the Tech Area." She took my hand and pulled me out onto the porch.

My mom hadn't been through our front door in three months, but I didn't say anything. We sat on the porch, muffled in darkness. We listened. Sure enough we heard and then saw three large trucks and a dozen or so cars pulling away from the Tech Area.

"They're moving it," said my mother. "They must be ready to give the old girl a whirl."

"What do you mean?" I asked.

But my mom just muttered, "Top secret. Top secret."

We went back inside. My mom began to search the kitchen drawers. I was speechless. She was moving. She was talking. She was almost like her old self.

Finally, she found what she was looking for. A map of New Mexico. She had bought it in Santa Fe, the very first day we arrived, just like any tourist visiting a new place.

She spread the map on the dining room table. With a pencil, she began to cross off areas until the map looked scarred and confusing. She put her head in her hands. "I'm going back to bed."

The next day, she pored over the map some more. She asked me again and again if I had heard anything unusual around town, any rumors, any news. I told her everything I knew. I told her what Dad had said to me before leaving. She looked at the map again, then she smiled. With her pencil, she drew a circle.

"It must be," she said.

I looked on the map. She had circled an area in New Mexico far south of us called the Jornada del Muerto.

"What does that mean?" I asked.

"It means the Journey of Death," she answered. "Now the only question is *when?*"

31

The Day the World Ended

That night I dreamed about Eleanor. She was standing in a beautiful green field, tossing a ball high into the air and catching it perfectly every time it fell. She was smiling and laughing. All of a sudden, she let the ball drop and turned to me. "You should have come with me," she said.

Someone was shaking me. I came awake slowly. It was my mom. She was standing next to my bed, dressed, with her coat on.

"We have to get up," she said. Was this still part of the dream? "Really, Hazel. I'm not joking. We don't have much time."

Time. Time. "What time is it?" I asked. All I wanted to do was sleep.

"One o'clock."

"In the morning? One o'clock in the morning? Why are we getting up?"

"Would you like to see the sun rise twice in one day? It's reason enough to lose a little sleep. Come on. The car is already packed."

"What car?"

"Jim's."

"Mr. Talbot's? Mr. Talbot's car? We can't take Mr. Talbot's car."

"He won't mind. He's off the Hill. And we'll be back before he is."

"We still can't take his car!" I insisted. For some reason, I was getting dressed the whole time I was arguing.

"We really don't have time to talk," said my mom. "I left the car running."

"Mom. I'm not kidding." By now I had my blue jeans and sweater on, but I was still fumbling with my socks and shoes. "We can't just take Mr. Talbot's car without asking."

"Oh Hazel," she said. And her voice sounded brighter than it had for months. "Tonight we can do anything!" She twirled me around as if we were dancing a reel. "Because tomorrow the world is going to end!"

"What are you talking about?" The knot of fear in my stomach that I'd been carrying around all summer tightened. Why was my mother so different all of a sudden? What had happened? What was *going* to happen?

"You'll know soon enough."

"I'm not going. You can't make me steal a car!" I was holding one shoe in my hand, and I let it drop with a loud thud to let her know I meant business.

"Oh, Hazel," said my mom, sounding disappointed. "With or without you, *I'm* going. But I really wanted you to come."

I could see in her eyes—those eyes that almost looked like my mother's eyes—that *she* was the one who meant business. And I had promised my dad that I would take care of her. I had promised. That would have been enough to make me follow her into the night in a stolen car. What she said next sealed my fate.

"Besides, don't you want to solve the mystery of the gadget? Tonight, you'll get all the answers you've been searching for."

That was that. I put on my shoe and we left the house. But as we pulled away in the green-and-white De Soto, I couldn't help thinking that stealing Mr. Talbot's car was becoming a habit.

The night air was cold even though it was July, and I found myself wishing I'd brought an extra sweater. As if she read my mind, my mom reached into the back seat and pulled out an old cotton blanket. Looking back, I saw she had packed two more blankets and a basket with a thermos sticking out.

"It's tonight," she said. "I stayed up listening, and I heard at least four cars pulling out. Eleanor Jette's Packard left about twenty minutes ago."

At the East Gate, the guard spent an extra-long time checking our passes. He examined our car carefully and wrote down a detailed description of the vehicle. I couldn't help thinking, *if he only knew the car was stolen!* But finally, he handed back our passes and lifted the gate.

"Seems like an awful lotta wives going off-site tonight," he said "What's goin' on? A sale at Macy's?" He chuckled at his own joke. It was the first and last time I ever heard one of the gate guards laugh.

"That's what *we'd* like to know," answered my mother.

We drove the first hour in silence. At first, we went down into the canyon, but then we began to climb. I couldn't even see the turns in the road. We seemed to be driving straight into pitch black.

After two hours, we reached a summit. It was even colder here, and we wrapped the remaining two blankets around us as we huddled in the front seat. My mom opened the thermos and the steaming, rich smell of hot chocolate filled the car.

"South is that way," she said, as much to herself as to me. She checked her watch. "But it's not even three o'clock yet. We'll have to wait an hour. Maybe two."

A gathering storm of anxiety was collecting in the pit of my stomach. What was going to happen? Why did my mom say the world was going to end? Was this the test that was going to set the air on fire? I tried to think of an escape plan. Where could we hide? Was there a cave nearby? Would that protect us? I had promised to take care of my mom. How could I? I took a vow, then and there. No matter what, I wouldn't let her out of my sight.

We sat in silence, surrounded by darkness.

I don't know if it was the lateness of the hour or the pitch black all around us or just my stomach full of hot chocolate, but I must have fallen asleep. I woke up with a start just as the first glow of dawn appeared over the ridge of the hill. The light was gray, and I could hardly make out anything but dark silhouettes. My feet were both asleep, tucked under me, and they throbbed and prickled as I stretched out my legs. That's when I noticed that my mom wasn't next to me anymore.

An icy cold knife sliced through my body. I had lost her. It had been my job to keep her safe, and I had lost her. What would my father say?

I opened the door and swung my legs to the ground, but they wouldn't hold me up for the pain. I kicked and slapped them impatiently, until I almost cried. As soon as I could stand it, I stepped out of the car and staggered forward. Instinctively, I headed for higher ground.

I was within twenty feet of the highest ridge when I caught sight of my mom. At first I thought she was a part of the rock, she stood so still, nothing more than a black shape against the dawning sky. But then, in the dim light, I could see her—the long braid and the familiar Diamond-in-the-Rough pattern on the quilt that was draped around her shoulders. But she didn't move. She seemed frozen.

That's when I fell. I must have tripped on something, or maybe I was just being my usual clumsy self. But I landed with a thud that sounded ten times louder in all that silence. Before I could even get up, my mom was by my side.

"Are you all right?" she asked. I nodded. "I shouldn't have brought you here. It was the wrong thing to do. I was just so sure that this would be the morning. I had one of my feelings. But it's almost five-thirty. And still so cold. I'm sorry. I shouldn't have done this to you."

"I don't mind," I said. "It's nice to be with you. Out of the house. We could at least stay to see the sun rise. We haven't done that in a long time."

We both turned toward the horizon, where the ground meets the sky. The sun hadn't yet risen over the mountains, and I could still just barely make out the shapes of the rocks and trees around us. I turned to ask my mother a question. And that's when it happened.

A flash of light a thousand times brighter than the sun. It was as if the world had been electrocuted. I could suddenly, instantly, see every branch on the tree behind my mother. The mountains were a brilliant, burning red—as though they had suddenly burst into flame. The outline of my mother's body looked as though it had been cut out with a razor, and I could see every single line on her face, every hair that framed her head. It was as if a photographer's bulb had suddenly exploded on the mountain top. Everything was sharper and brighter and more real than it had ever been.

And then it was dark again, darker than before. I could hardly see anything. All the shapes were black. All were blurred. I reached out groping for my mother, even though I knew she stood only a few feet away. I thought I had gone blind. In a panic, I grabbed her arm. And then I heard the rumble. Low and steady, growing stronger. It sounded like far-off thunder, rolling toward us. But it didn't stop. It went on and on and on. For seconds, minutes. And then it died away.

And everything was just as it had been before.

My mother sat down heavily on the cold hard ground, pulling me down with her.

"It is born," she said.

"What do you mean?" I asked. But she wouldn't answer. The way she had said "It is born" sounded like she was talking about *death*. I felt the way I did when I saw Severo's drowned body. The way I did when I read about the boy in Hamburg. I felt surrounded by death.

But where was death? Not here, on this hilltop with my mother. Where was it? I couldn't see it. I couldn't touch it. But I felt it as surely as I felt my warm breath on my icy face. It had me in its grip.

I stood up, trying to shake free. I pulled on my mother's arm. "We should go home. I want to go home."

She allowed me to lead her back to the car, but when I sat her behind the wheel, she wouldn't drive. I begged. I cried. She didn't seem to hear me. It was like she was asleep with her eyes open.

I got her out of the front seat and settled her in the back. I tucked Granny's quilt around her and then folded the other two blankets and piled them on the driver's seat. I climbed on top of the pile and prayed that I would remember everything that Eleanor taught me. About being brave. About having faith. About how to shift from neutral to first.

It took us four hours to get home. The speedometer never topped ten miles an hour. There was only one glitch on the whole trip. On one turn, heading down into a canyon, the car slid a little on some loose sand. I panicked and slammed on the brakes, and when the car finally stopped, we were off the road, with one tire hanging in thin air over a hundred-foot drop.

"Damn it, Eleanor," I cursed. "Why didn't you show me how to shift into reverse?"

But I figured it out. I guess Eleanor was right. I'm a natural.

The guard's eyes bugged out when I pulled up to the gate.

"My mom felt sick just a mile back, so I had to drive," I said. "I better get her home. She needs to get in bed."

"You know how to drive?" he asked, handing back our passes in a hurry.

"Oh, sure, I've been doing it for years."

And I felt like I had.

32

No More Secrets

All that morning, I stood on our balcony watching the activity below. The kids were shooed outside to play. The mothers traveled in troops from one house to the next. I saw Mrs. Jette race down the street to hug Mrs. Bainbridge, kicking up dust as she ran. They whispered and made wild arm gestures; they could hardly keep from dancing a jig in the street. Then Mrs. Embley and Mrs. Shneiderman came running out of their houses, and the four of them linked arms and skipped out of sight. From another balcony, a mom holding a baby flashed the V for victory sign as the dancing moms passed below.

I could have gone out into the street. I could have asked any of the kids playing stickball or jacks or tag what was going on. What was the news. But I didn't. In the year-and-a-half I'd been on the Hill, I'd figured one thing out: The dads knew everything, the moms knew something, and the kids knew nothing.

My mom had promised me all the answers to my questions about the gadget. But instead, I seemed to have more questions than ever. And my mom wouldn't talk.

She hadn't said a word since the light flashed on top of the mountain. She was in bed, but not asleep. I heard her restless movements as she rearranged the sheets, beat the pillows, and tossed and turned.

We hadn't eaten any breakfast. I looked in the refrigerator in the hope of pulling together a lunch. I found some cheese and coleslaw and half a loaf of bread. It would do.

"Mom?" I asked, poking my head into her dim bedroom. I felt like a mole, small and blind in the dark. "Do you want some lunch?"

No answer.

"I could heat up some Campbell's. I think we have tomato and rice. Do you want me to get you a bowl?"

No answer.

I backed out of the room. I closed my mother's door. I sat in the living room on my mother's rocker and waited. I would wait forever if I had to. Wait for my dad to come home.

It was just after three when I heard his steps on the porch. He walked slowly and heavily. When he opened the door, he wasn't the least surprised to find me stationed there, waiting.

The words tumbled out of my mouth. "I want to know now. Everything. Absolutely everything. I know the kids aren't supposed to know. The kids are never supposed to know anything. But *I am not a kid.*"

He hadn't even had a chance to put down the paper sack that held his dirty clothes and empty thermos. His eyes drooped as if he hadn't slept in weeks, and his shoulders sagged. His clothes were wrinkled, and his shirt was untucked. He looked like a runover piece of garbage.

"Before I say anything," said my dad. "I need to know one thing. How's your mother?"

"She stopped talking. Ever since we saw the flash of light. She won't say a word."

"You saw it? All the way here?" His scientific mind was instantly engaged.

"No. Not here. We were on top of a mountain. We drove about two hours south of here and went to the top of a mountain."

"You saw it! Almost two hundred miles away and you saw it." He seemed amazed and horrified by this. "It *is* a monster." He sat down on the couch. "Where is she?"

"In bed. I think she might be sleeping. She's been quiet now for the last hour."

"Sleep," he said, rubbing his eyes. "It sounds so wonderful. So impossible."

He sat on the couch and leaned over to untie his shoes, but his fingers fumbled as if they weren't attached properly to his body.

"Let me do that," I said a little crossly, though I didn't mean to sound that way.

"Thanks, Hazelnut." He slumped back on the couch. "I know you're not a little kid. Somewhere, somehow, I don't know exactly when, you crossed the line. If you ask me, thirteen is a little too young to have done that, but what's done is done. You're a grownup now. One of us. So listen carefully to what I say. And promise that you will not repeat this information to anyone, anywhere, until I say it's okay."

I nodded my head solemnly.

"You understand nuclear fission. You know that when

a reaction occurs, a great deal of heat and energy are released."

"Yes! Yes!" I had no patience.

My father, the scientist, had infinite patience. "Here on the Hill, we've spent the last two years making a bomb fueled by nuclear fission. An atomic bomb. A bomb so powerful and devastating that it makes every other bomb look like a pop gun. You can't even imagine the power of this thing. You were almost two hundred miles away from the test site, and you still saw the light. Imagine if you'd been only twenty miles away. Or ten. Imagine if you'd been at ground zero."

My mind raced, trying to fit in this new piece to the puzzle. The puzzle of our lives on the Hill. "It's not a rocket? Or a ship? Or even a submarine?" My voice faltered. How could this be? "You made a bomb? A bomb to kill people?"

"It's going to end the war. It's going to save hundreds of thousands of American lives." He stared at the ceiling. "And God help us. Maybe we'll never have to actually use it. Maybe we can stage another test and show the Japanese what a terrible weapon we've made. Then they'll surrender, and no one will have to die."

But I couldn't believe that. No, I thought. It *will* be used. And so many will die. I remembered the rolling thunder that wouldn't stop. I remembered the flash of light. Hundreds of thousands will die.

A bomb. It was so crude, so elementary, so destructive. There was nothing beautiful in a bomb. And what would Mom say?

My dad looked closely at my face. He could tell what I was thinking, and it hurt him. He wanted to convince me. He wanted to win me over to his side. "Hazel, think of what this means. This bomb means the end of all wars. There'll never be another war again. No one would dare start a war with a weapon like this in our hands. Finally, there will be peace for all time."

We sat in silence. What else was there to say? Thousands of people were going to die because of my father. But thousands would be saved because of him. What kind of mathematical equation was that?

"Mom knows, doesn't she?" I asked. "She's always known. From the very beginning. All the other moms have had to guess and wonder. But Mom has always known everything about the gadget, hasn't she?"

"Your mom and I are like two parts of the same body. The head can't lie to the heart anymore than the heart can lie to the head. I had to tell her everything. It wasn't a choice. I just had to tell her. Now, I wish I hadn't. But then again, your mom's a pretty smart lady. Dollars to doughnuts she would have figured it out on her own." He put an arm around my shoulder. "Can I tell you something crazy? Sometimes, I think she can read my mind?"

We laughed. It was the first time I'd laughed in days. Or weeks? I couldn't even remember.

"Oh, Dad," I said, hugging him around his neck. "Are we finally going home?"

"On the first bus, Hazelnut. On the very first bus."

33

The Crooked Path

We've been home for more than six months now. It's spring, and the trees in Montclair are so beautiful. All green and dripping wet and newly born. The trees on the Hill never looked like that.

Dad just went back to teaching at the university this week. When we first got home, they offered him a six-month sabbatical, and he took it. It's been slow and strange, settling into our old house, just the two of us. But now he's teaching again, back where he belongs. He's got a light load this semester so he can be home every afternoon when I get out of school.

The kids at school still ask me questions. Millions of questions. What was it like in Los Alamos? Did you ever touch plutonium? Were there any German spies hiding there? Did you ever shoot a gun? And where's your mom? I get that question a lot. How come your mom doesn't live at home with you?

I just tell them whatever. Whatever I feel like saying. Mostly it's the truth. But every once in a while, I say that we ate plutonium soup and we all carried guns with us and my mom was a secret agent so we had to turn her over to the authorities. But mostly I tell the truth. Really.

At least as much as I know. We never did find out if there were really spies on the Hill. Maybe that's something we'll never know.

And I'm back to being the smart one in class. There was no way out of that one. I've been in school with these same kids since we were in kindergarten. They know who I am. And I know who I am, at least more than I did when we set out for Los Alamos two years ago. The truth of it is, I'm *not* as smart as I thought I was. It's like my mom said—there's a lot to learn in this world.

My mom, meanwhile, is at Cranmore, which is only a forty-five minute bus ride away, so Dad and I visit her almost every day. She's doing okay. It's peaceful out there. Lots of trees and a lake and doctors and nurses to take care of her all the time. She likes it, although she told me the other day that she misses the Sangre de Cristos. I didn't tell her, but so do I.

Sometimes, she almost sounds like her old self. Like when she talks about joining the peace movement. She's been writing a lot of letters to Mrs. Bainbridge, who was one of the moms on the Hill. Mrs. Bainbridge is a Quaker, and she's leading a group that wants to make sure the bomb will never be used again. My mom wants to help.

She's not her old self yet. Maybe she never will be. But this weekend, she's going to spend all day Saturday here. And Dad says she might be able to come home for Easter. Maybe for good.

The war is over, and nothing is the same. There's a big

strike going on right now with the railroads. People want higher wages. There aren't enough jobs to go around now that all the GIs have come home. And a lot of the women who worked in the factories don't want to give up their jobs and go back to housework. And suddenly, everyone wants to go to college! It's what the government promised all the servicemen.

All our neighbors say Dad is a hero. Mrs. Wyatt, who lives across the street, told me, "I'm glad we got the bomb before the Russkies!" But Dad says it's only a matter of time before the Russians make an atomic bomb. And then it will be like being at war all the time. Eleanor says the Russians aren't smart enough to build the bomb. "Trust me," she says. "I know what I'm talking about." I'm going to visit Eleanor this summer. My dad says I'm old enough to take the train to Chicago all by myself.

So things are pretty different and a little mixed up. But that's okay. If everything was exactly the way it had been before the war, then I wouldn't fit in anymore. Because *I'm* different. I'm not a kid anymore. I don't look at the world the same way.

I got a letter from Simon last week. He's planning to go to Harvard in the fall and says I can visit him there anytime I want. He says the two of us would make a terrific team if we ever decide to put our heads together. He says that scientists are starting to build machines as big as houses that can add numbers faster than the smartest human being on earth, and he wants to be in on that. Maybe I'll do that, too.

All I know is I want to be in on *something* big. Something even bigger than the atomic bomb. I can't say what it is, but when it comes along, I'll know it. I'll listen to the voice in my heart, and I'll know it's the right thing to do with my life. Because that's what I learned on the Hill. There are choices you make. And some of those choices lead you in the right direction, and some of them take you off course. But you can always find your way back, as long as you remember to ask yourself those questions my mom taught me when I was just a little kid.

Meanwhile, I've been keeping my eye on the horizon. That's where all our possibilities lie. My mom's right. It's the most beautiful place on earth.

Author's note

From 1939 to 1945, World War II raged across four continents. Three nations with imperialistic desires—Germany, Italy, and Japan—attacked their neighbors, drawing more and more countries into the conflict. Before the end of the war, battles were fought in Europe, Africa, Australia, China, and the Pacific Island region.

The rulers in all three aggressor nations wanted more land for their countries. Germany's ruler was Adolf Hitler, leader of the Nazi Party. The Nazis believed in a separate race of German people who were tall, blond, and blue-eyed. They called these people German Aryans and believed they were superior to all other races. The Nazis also believed that Germany should rule Europe and that all Jews should be exterminated.

Italy's ruler was Benito Mussolini, leader of the Fascist Party. He hoped to restore Italy to its former glory by creating a new Roman Empire in North Africa.

In Japan, Emperor Hirohito ruled, but his decisions were strongly controlled by Japan's Prime Minister, Hideki Tojo. Tojo was the leader of the promilitary Nationalist Party. He wanted to capture land in Asia and the Pacific Ocean.

During the 1930s, all three nations began their campaigns of aggression. The United States, however, refused to join in the fighting until December 7, 1941, when the Japanese bombed the U.S. naval base at Pearl Harbor, Hawaii. The surprise attack killed 2,400 Americans, sank 18 ships, and destroyed 292 aircraft. The next day, President Franklin Delano Roosevelt led Congress to declare war on Japan, Germany, and Italy. Within months, U.S. soldiers joined Allied forces fighting in countries across Europe and North Africa, as well as in the Pacific.

Just before the war began, German physicists made one of the most important scientific discoveries of the century: *nuclear fission*. This discovery led to further experiments. In 1942, the Italian physicist Enrico Fermi, who had fled Fascist Italy and was living in exile in the United States, engineered the world's first sustained nuclear *chain reaction*.

Some scientists were alarmed by these discoveries, because they realized nuclear fission could be used to create a new and terrible weapon: an atomic bomb. Several scientists, including physicist Albert Einstein, wrote a letter to President Roosevelt pointing out this possibility.

With Europe in turmoil and Hitler on the rise, it was a terrifying prospect that such a weapon might join Germany's arsenal. In 1942, U.S. Army intelligence reported that the Germans were working furiously on building an atomic bomb. In response, the army assigned General Leslie Groves to lead the Manhattan Project, the code name for the Allied effort to build the bomb.

General Groves selected American physicist J. Robert Oppenheimer to direct the scientific work of the project. Their first task was to choose a site for the laboratory—a site that was remote and secure, but that had enough water and electricity to power a lab. Oppenheimer chose

Los Alamos, an isolated mesa hidden between the Jemez and Sangre de Cristo mountains in northern New Mexico. As early as 1943, he began to assemble his team of scientists, which included many of the most brilliant minds of the century. Some were Americans, but many were world-renowned scientists who had been forced to flee their home countries of Italy, Germany, Denmark, Poland, and Hungary because of Hitler's ruthless advance.

Both Groves and Oppenheimer understood that the scientists they recruited would work most effectively if accompanied by their families. And so Los Alamos became a strange hybrid: part army base, part scientific lab, and part suburban community. The town had a school, a hospital, a day-care center, a movie theater, a drugstore, a laundromat, a radio station, and a grocery store. There were square dances, church services, ski trips, skating parties, and community theater productions. In one sense, Los Alamos could have been Anytown, USA. And yet the town was shrouded in secrecy. The residents had no official address. They carried driver's licenses with no names. And they were not allowed to vote in any local, state, or national elections. They lived in a town that—as far as the rest of the world knew—did not exist.

On April 12, 1945, President Roosevelt died. Vice-President Harry S Truman took the presidential oath of office and assumed the role of commander in chief of the U.S. armed forces. Until that day, Truman had never heard of the atomic bomb.

On July 16, 1945, at a test site in the New Mexican

desert 200 miles south of Los Alamos, the world's first atomic bomb was detonated. The success of this test astounded the scientists and army personnel who witnessed it. No one had ever seen such destructive power unleashed by a single weapon. But the bomb remained a tightly held military secret. Only those associated with the Manhattan Project knew that a new weapon had been born.

At this point, the war against Germany was over, but the fighting continued in the Pacific region. The battles in this arena were fought island by island, with enormous casualties on both sides. Although the United States was clearly marching toward victory, the Japanese government refused to surrender. Throughout the summer of 1945, the United States prepared to launch a full-scale invasion of Japan, fearing that the death toll for American soldiers would be staggering.

The invasion never happened. On August 6, 1945, the United States dropped an atomic bomb on the Japanese city of Hiroshima. One hundred thousand people were killed immediately by the explosion. Another 100,000 died from radiation poisoning over the next five years. The city itself was demolished. On August 9, the United States dropped a second atomic bomb on the city of Nagasaki. One hundred and forty thousand people died as a result of that bombing. Five days later, Japan surrendered, and World War II came to an end.

More than fifty years after the only atomic bombs ever used in warfare were dropped, people still debate whether it was right or wrong for the Los Alamos scientists to create such a weapon. Herbert York, a scientist who worked on the Manhattan Project during World War II, often lectures to young students today. He likes to begin his lectures by saying,

> The first thing you knew about World War II is how it came out. And that's the last thing I knew about World War II. It took me four years to find out how it was going to come out. The first thing you knew about the atomic bomb is that we used it to kill a lot of people in Hiroshima. And that's the last thing I knew about the atomic bomb.

Fifty-five million soldiers and civilians were killed during World War II. It was the bloodiest war the world has ever seen.

What Is Nuclear Fission?

Everything on earth is made up of atoms. Air, water, earth—all can be broken down and understood as combinations of different atoms.

Each atom is made up of three kinds of particles: protons, neutrons, and electrons. The number of protons, neutrons, and electrons can be thought of as a "recipe" for each atom. For example, a helium atom—one of the simplest atoms on earth—has two protons, two neutrons, and two electrons.

Most atoms are stable. They don't tend to fall apart or transform into other atoms. In other words, they don't spontaneously change their recipes.

Some larger atoms—such as uranium—are unstable. Uranium (in one of its forms) has 92 protons and 143 neutrons. When a uranium atom is bombarded by a neutron, it can split in two, creating two smaller, lighter atoms. This process of splitting apart is called *nuclear fission*.

Two things happen in nuclear fission: The reaction gives off energy (mostly in the form of heat), and it releases more neutrons. These additional neutrons hit *other* uranium atoms, which may cause them to split apart. And so the process continues—a cycle of splitting atoms, releasing neutrons, and thus splitting more atoms. This continuing process is called a *chain reaction*. As long as the chain reaction continues, the process gives off energy. Atomic bombs use the energy of chain reactions to create their destructive power.